Hope Points North

—◆◆◆—

Robert Douglas Spetta

This is a work of fiction. All events and characters described in this book are imaginary.

ISBN: 0615948103
ISBN 13: 9780615948102
Library of Congress Control Number: 2014930192
Star Flight Security Press, Ronkonkoma, NY

Hope Points North
Robert Douglas Spetta

I definitely am not a writer. The longest piece I ever wrote was a twenty-page, slightly plagiarized research paper on ionic bonds as a sophomore in college, and that was over thirty years ago. Nonetheless I am putting these words down because I feel that I have a story to tell. I'm afraid that otherwise this sliver of my past will vanish thirty or, if I'm really lucky, forty years from now when I go to meet my indeterminate Maker, on the top of Mount Vesuvius.

Thankfully I don't have any physical ailments or maladies that are about to foreshorten my insignificant life. However, I am going through a personal crisis that requires weekly visits to a psychologist so that I can discover what is broken in my head. During times of stress my formative childhood years surface to explain my reactions to the here and now. So I write to remember, to sleep, to have sex again with my wife, and not fall into the voyeuristic void of watching TV.

This is my personal story. It is an interesting tale to hear while sitting around the dinner table or reminiscing during a reunion, but that's about it. I certainly don't want to see some over paid pretenders make a mockery of the chronicle in the name of art or money. No, that is not what this story is about. I am writing it down simply so that I can recall the fifties and sixties when men in white space suits and bubble helmets flew rocket ships to the moon.

It seems that the past is always better remembered than experienced. Maybe someday one of my children or grandchildren will find this diary and see how it was to live in a vanished America. I write about what I know because I'm not a good enough liar to make up stories. I wish I were a Hemmingway or a Vonnegut, but I'm not. In the end I must rely on my story of the past because I'm tired of taking pills, and I'm tired of sitting around with nothing on my mind, and I'm tired of being tired. So I write.

I

My therapist says it will be good for me to sit down and write after losing my job. It is very tough to lose a job when you are forty-seven years old too old to hire and too young to retire. Caught in the trap of a bad economy and an indulgent lifestyle, I, like others of my generation, turned into overextended consumers. Our parents never seemed to entrench themselves in such quagmires. They were just happy to enjoy life at home.

Home from the foxholes in Europe or the jungles of the South Pacific, satisfied with a roof over their heads and some kids running around in the yard. Home was a sacred place where mothers stayed and fathers returned after working in a job that would support their families for the rest of their lives. Home was simple and safe, a place, sadly, that probably will never be known again in America.

I sit here staring at a device that at one time was an invaluable tool for navigators of planet Earth, but that with the advent of GPS has become a technological relic. Mr. Conrad's compass has always been a source of inspiration and strength to me, and I must tell how my tool of Nordic kings came into my possession before I am obliged to sell this historical instrument to pay my mortgage. It is a sacrifice I thought I would never have to contemplate, but in times of global recession desperate acts become more commonplace, not just for me but for all of us who bought into the American Dream based on the unsubstantiated magic of easy credit.

I suppose I could sell the compass on E-bay to some faraway stranger in China, Japan, or India, but somehow that doesn't seem quite right. I would rather an American had this instrument, even at a financial loss to myself. I therefore have hatched a plan that even in these hard economic times just might work. A museum of flight might want this historical artifact before it too follows the flow of our capital overseas.

Now that I have time on my hands, I find myself procrastinating and driving to places of my past. I ride in my car, just as I once rode my bike, until something interesting catches my attention. Eventually I find myself back in the place where the compass first entered my life. These empty streets were once filled with woods; now they are devoid of life, all in the name of suburban progress.

The trees have vanished completely. The majestic gray smooth skinned trunks of beech trees, wrinkled brown bases of century old oaks, and even the long straight up strength of the locust trees have been pulverized into mulch and razed for firewood. The woods have been replaced by mini-mansions surrounded by manicured lawns that leave no room for the natural world. What remains is a sad contrast to the splendor that had been in this spot for thousands of years.

We were the last Algonquians to walk under the canopy of leaves that led to the sea. In the sixties a baby-boomers adolescence was a time of active imagination, not one encumbered by the seduction of video games or a fear of molesters, a time when a kid's mission was to be out the back door after breakfast and home by dinner. What happened in the interim was more or less up to you. The consequences of decisions were learned independently by trial and error.

I stand in this spot with compass in hand searching for those lessons of the past, a location where the woods were my classroom. It was a place where the summer breezes of sea air flowed over and into my body, where packs of children and dogs roamed freely past unfenced property lines and played games according to our own rules. At that time and in that world, no matter how precariously perched on the brink of nuclear annihilation we were, life always seemed to make perfect sense from the moment we rose to play outside in the morning, until our exhausted heads hit our pillows at night.

The reason why I stand here is that the memory of my youth is the only trail left for me to travel. As an adult I bottomed out long ago. My life had become a hole into which I found myself sinking deeper and deeper. No matter how hard I searched, there seemed not to be the slightest glimmer or ray of hope from above, and because of this fact I find myself revisiting this now profane location.

That is why I parked here as a stranger or interloper in a place I once knew so well, searching for some comfort in memories. As I stared at the ghostly remnants of trees that had once constituted an unbroken forest, and as I contemplated the waters meandering through all the curves and bends of a seacoast tributary that once had been mine alone to fish. I returned to a time when I watched the tidal flow, doing what the nearby inlet's waters have done faithfully for the past ten thousand years.

As I contemplated the past, my gaze is momentarily interrupted by a flutter of curtains in a home's windows. Evidently I have parked here too long because the stranger who lives in the house that used to be my spot of land has become alarmed. If I remain parked here for more than ten minutes, I might become a source of alarm. Yet this current person's apprehensions don't really matter because this will always be my place where a bend in the creek meets a sandbar in the middle as the water flows out to the sea.

Part One

II

The Beginning

We had slept on the ground all night, and our fire had reduced itself to dusty charcoal and a few orange embers. The evening had been typical for October, warm air during the day but bracingly cool at night, foreshadowing the winter to come on Long Island. Though we were only in seventh grade, we were allowed to camp out in the woods overnight. Our fathers and mothers had total confidence that we would be home by morning. We were all white kids whose parents had fled the urban multiracial centers to embrace the American Dream of a suburban home with a yard.

This had always been our spot to camp. From our vantage point we could watch the movement of the tides as the sea's salt water flowed in and out of our creek. When the morning light broke through the darkness, the tainted smell of muck and decay indicated that the tide was low, and an elongated white sandbar, caressed on either side by the outgoing tide, became our focus.

We were a motley group, true misfits in our school class, and because of this commonality we had become fast friends. Our friendship came about for two simple reasons. The primary bond was our status as outsiders in the caste system of teenagers, but more importantly it was our ability to make each other laugh. We had found each other out of necessity, and this made our fraternity strong.

Charlie Fairchild always slept late, his outline in the sleeping bag not stirring until well after first light. His dad was of all things a nuclear scientist at the federal facility of Brookhaven Lab. At the time it was important to identify what your father did because your father's job defined what you were, and in his case the genetics rang true for Charlie.

Skinny and pale with red straw-like hair, Charlie had the distinction of being the smartest kid in school. His family had moved to Northern Shores from Chicago about five years ago, and Charlie still retained a Midwestern accent. Charlie's greatest asset was his scientific thought process, and he was always coming up with some sort of experiment that was interesting to our group. Whether he was studying the forces of erosion with a garden hose or dissecting the digestive system of a recently caught fish, he added a methodical approach to our outings that usually kept Teddy and me on the verge of getting into trouble.

Though smart, Charlie was socially inept. He never played sports, rarely spoke in class, and was obsessed with toy soldiers. He wore horn-rimmed glasses with lenses so thick that they distorted his pale grey eyes, and without them he was as sightless as an earthworm burrowing through the soil. Had it not been for Teddy and myself, Charlie would probably have spent most of his time reading history books or scientific papers in the damp corners of his basement.

When we went camping, I was always the second one to arise. My pilot father had always instilled the necessity of time schedules into my soul, so to sleep past a certain hour was impossible for me. About the only thing I can say for myself otherwise is that I was the average one of the bunch. I was never the last or the first to be picked at a football or baseball game. My school performance was not exactly what one could call stellar, my grades being good enough to keep me from getting grounded, but not high enough for accolades or the honor society. I didn't know what I wanted to be when I got older, and my life just seemed to flow around the short term matters of thinking about girls' breasts or what I was going to eat for my next meal.

On the fleeting occasions when I did focus on my life's objectives, my obsessions centered around three things: comic books, fishing, and Indians. Had it not been for the crime-fighting worlds of Spiderman and Superman, I doubt that I would ever have learned to read, and probably to this date I would still be sounding out words while scanning the morning paper. Aside from this benefit, the angst of Spiderman's teenage dilemmas always kept me enthralled with this teenage superhero's life. Superman, on the other hand, captivated me by his power. It was comforting for me to think that there was a humanoid out there who could defeat any evil, even one as great as the Communist threat that might blow my inane existence to a fiery thermonuclear conclusion at any moment.

Fishing seemed to satisfy an uncontrollable primal urge for me. One part hunting and one part contemplation, it is an obsession that takes perseverance because there are times when nothing can be caught. Many of my waking hours were spent casting lures along the edges of streams or into the currents in an attempt to fool a fish into a bogus meal. I persisted cast after cast until I experienced the thrill of a strike and hauled a fish to shore.

However, as important as these preoccupations were in my life, my ultimate obsession was how I was going to become an

Indian. Forget the fact that I was white and that my ancestors were the McKellar's of Northern European descent. Never mind that I didn't know how to ride a horse and that I had never been further west than Harrisburg, Pennsylvania. These were just minor technicalities. My secrete passion was somehow to find that hidden wilderness still left in the United States where buffalo roamed freely and I could grow up to become a Sioux warrior.

Theodore Roosevelt Hooker, the third member of our clan, was always the first one to awaken when we camped. Teddy was the wild one of the group. His father, a Navy pilot, was MIA, shot down while flying over the DMZ, somewhere over the rice paddies and jungles of NAM. Because our country had to stop the Communist dominoes from falling, a line had been drawn in this little backwater of a country 12,000 miles away where men were sent to die for the cause of democracy. At home the streets churned, college students protested, and growing discontent seeped into the evening news with death tallies, draft-card burnings, and violence, making mothers and wives ask "Why?"

Teddy's mother could not find an explanation for why her naval-officer husband, who could fly a jet at supersonic speeds and land his plane on an aircraft carrier bobbing in the China Sea, had vanished without a trace. In order to find an answer to the inexplicable, she did as people often do and turned to God to solve her conundrum. From this calamity arose a man of faith, a self-proclaimed conduit to God, who provided Ted's attractive mother with the slightest glimmer of hope so that she could go on with a life that had seemed to lose all meaning upon her husband's disappearance.

Caleb Lovejoy was an evangelical minister who stepped in to fill the void for Teddy's mother after three years of despair and empty responses from the Pentagon to her inquiries. The pastor was a comfort to his mother, and in her emotional state she was easy prey for a man who used Jesus as a tool for a personal end.

Lovejoy disliked Teddy as much as was Christianly possible because of the boy's refusal to believe that it was God's will his father was gone, and Lovejoy also recognized Teddy's suspicions about the true reasons behind the minister's consolatory visits to his mother. Teddy knew that his father was still alive, and no preacher was going to convince him to the contrary, no matter what his mother believed.

It was not unusual for Teddy to have a bruise on some part of his body. Some said that these contusions were the result of his rough-and-tumble games, but whispers had floated about the community involving Reverend Lovejoy. Wherever the bruises came from, the boy never revealed their origin.

Teddy was tall and thin with a mop of dark wavy hair that was never combed. He smelled of cat because of his mother's recent preoccupation with breeding mongrel cats. His clothes were always covered with feline hair of some hue, and animal dander was his constant companion. His upper lip was just beginning to show the start of mustache growth, which only added to his unkempt appearance. Most people chose to avoid Ted, a reception that had hardened the boy far too early in his short and troubled life.

However, this is not what made Teddy so special. Theodore Roosevelt Hooker's most amazing trait was his total lack of respect for authority in any form. Teachers, parents, policemen, bullies, Boy Scout leaders, and priests were all shown the same democratic contempt. It was not uncommon for Ted to be serving a sentence of detention for some misconduct during his waking hours. The terms "ingrate," "delinquent," "detrimental," and "atrocious" were often heard in association with his name, yet if Teddy liked you there was no better friend to have on the face of the planet.

For some strange reason my parents never seemed concerned about my relationship with Teddy. I don't know whether it was from lack of involvement on their part or whether they saw something in Teddy that most people didn't recognize, but never once did they prohibit me from socializing with this rapscallion. I could understand my father's lack of involvement because as a commercial airline pilot he was subject to long absences from home. However, my housewife mother seemed to show the same lack of interest when it came to Ted, and she treated him no differently than any of my other playmates.

About the only time Teddy was engaged or calm came when he was discussing his one true obsession in life, which was his dream of becoming an astronaut. Space saved Ted. While most kids our age were interested in baseball players and could spit out the stats of Mays or Mantle with relative ease, Teddy could have cared less about these figures. But when it came to the Mercury, Gemini, or fledgling Apollo space programs, he knew every aspect of each mission. His heroes were named Glenn, Shepard, Cooper, Schirra, and White.

He would spend hours by our campfire pontificating about each mission. One of the darkest times in Ted's life transpired when three Apollo One astronauts were tragically killed on January 27, 1967 during a launch-pad accident during a practice session. After the catastrophe Teddy hardly spoke for the next three days as he mourned his idols' deaths. Even with this setback and poor grades at school, there was no doubt in Ted's mind that he would grow up to become an astronaut. On one of our early-morning bivouacs, however, it seemed that space held little interest for Teddy.

Only half awake, my mind still in a fog, I watched him building something on the sandbar that had appeared from the receding waters overnight. To my untrained eye Ted appeared to be constructing an odd sandcastle, and I shouted down to him.

"Hey Teddy, whatcha making?"

"Come on down and you'll see," he replied.

"Need any help?" I asked.

"Maybe. Just come down here."

I kicked Charlie. "Wake up," I urged. "Teddy needs help building something."

Charlie barely stirred as his muffled voice rose from his sleeping bag. "Forget Ted. Let's go home to get something to eat. I'm hungry."

"I'm going down to the sandbar," I replied. "You can come if you want to. We can always get something to eat later." I then abruptly left him while he continued dozing.

The trail ran down the twenty-foot embankment of white birch trees to the water's reed-filled edge. The water felt cold as I slipped a toe and then an entire foot into the creek. I was never one to jump into the water all at once. Each step had to be a gradual immersion into the flowing saltwater. Meanwhile Teddy was absorbed in working on his sand masterpiece, not looking up from his creation as I swam over to the sandbar. Normally he would throw mud balls in my direction or dunk me as I swam to the bar, but today he was so enthralled by his project that he hardly noticed my crossing.

Upon my arrival I walked over to Ted. His concentration was unwavering on what I soon found out was not a castle or tower but a sand woman. Her two-dimensional face had primitively shaped features that displayed all the artistic mastery of a drunken first-grader. However, truly striking about the figure were her gargantuan breasts, so massive that they would probably require a size triple "J" brassiere. It was obvious that Teddy had been spending more time on that part of her anatomy than on others.

"What are you working on?" I asked.

With all the concentration of a Pollack or Picasso, Ted never looked up to answer. "A sand girl," he muttered.

"What's her name?"

Ted thought a moment. "Sandy."

"She's not right, you know."

My blasphemous comment diverted Ted from his work. "What do you mean she's not right?"

Drawing on my adolescent knowledge of the female anatomy gleaned from a highly worn September 1965 issue of *Playboy* I had concealed in my basement couch, I confidently stated, "She's missing a vagina."

Ted stood up, stepped back from his creation, and finally turned his attention away from her breasts and stared at her pelvis. He knew that I was correct in my critique of Sandy, for he had seen my precious copy of *Playboy* nearly as many times as I had. Our dilemma now became that of what item from a beach does one use to represent female genitalia. Ted began to scan the sandbar for artistic inspiration. He fumbled with some clamshells but quickly abandoned them.

His eureka moment came in the form of seaweed. True, it wasn't the consistency of pubic hair, and, yes, it was green in color, but Teddy, exercising artistic license, placed handfuls of the abundant plant in Sandy's crotch, where it seemed to suffice for our purposes. He then stood back and beamed with pride on his masterpiece.

"What do you think, Chris?"

"It's good, but she needs one more thing."

"What's that?" Ted asked.

"A birth canal," I replied.

"Why do we need that?"

"Because Mr. Woodland says so," I confidently stated.

"What's Woodland got to do with this?" Naturally Teddy hated Mr. Woodland.

"Because he's our health teacher, and he told us that children come out of there. She's a woman, isn't she?"

"Yeah."

"Well?" I prodded.

Monica Webber was the only girl in our class who was fully developed by the seventh grade. Although our cohort spent much of our time staring at her breasts and dreamed of one day fondling them, that was as close as we got to an encounter with the female anatomy. Neither Ted nor I had any vicarious reference points when it came to birth canals or vaginas, except for the one from which we emerged fourteen years ago.

"So do it," I urged.

"Do what?"

"Put it on her."

"That's alright. You can do it," Teddy answered.

"Hey, she's your creation."

"I know!" he snapped.

"Listen, you can't have a girl without a birth canal, so do it."

With some hesitation Ted walked over to Sandy and punched a hole between her legs. "There. She's done, birth canal and all." He stepped back, and we admired his work.

It was still early morning, but we could guess that it was around six o'clock. We walked around Sandy to see whether any other finishing touches were needed. "So what do you think?" Ted asked.

"Okay, I guess."

"Good."

Teddy shouted up to the campsite, "Hey Charlie, come on down. I need you to look at something."

Charlie popped his head up from the bushes, his shoulders draped in a sleeping bag as he reluctantly shuffled to the water's edge. "Listen guys," he said. "I want to go home. I'm really hungry."

Teddy shouted back to him, "Just come down here, you wimp! You have all day to sit around home."

Tossing his sleeping bag to the ground, Charlie tentatively walked down to the water's edge, waded into the creek, and began a breast stroke over to the bar. His weak swimming style reminded me of an old woman out for a Sunday dip. Charlie's pale body was already shivering as he walked over to the sand sculpture.

"Interesting," he said. "I thought you were making some sort of odd sand castle."

Much to my surprise Ted walked over to Charlie and said," She's all yours."

Charlie nervously pushed his smudged glasses up on the bridge of his nose. "She's all mine? What do you mean?"

"You get to do her. Chris and I already have done her, so now it's your chance."

"I will not!" Charlie retorted. "You're full of shit. There's no way you fornicated with that sand castle."

I ducked my head and tried to look in the other direction as Ted continued with his fabrication.

"No, it's all true. I mean, it was my idea first, but Chris said it sounded like a good idea that we both stick our dicks into Sandy, so technically we aren't virgins any more. That way, if you are ever with a girl like Monica Webber, she will think that you have experience."

"Yeah, girls always want experienced men," I chimed in.

"No, I don't buy it," Charlie said.

"It's true. Chris and I both shoved our wieners into Sandy's birth canal, so it's your turn. Otherwise you're not part of the club."

"The club?"

"Yeah, the Fucking Sandy Club," Ted explained.

Charlie glanced at Ted and then stared long and hard at me. He knew that Teddy was always up to some sort of mischief and that this "club" seemed a little odd, even for Teddy, but he could always trust me. He thus scrutinized me closely to see whether I was lying about my first sexual experience. Charlie's analytical brain was working overtime concerning his virginity and this silicon strumpet.

Being no fool, Charlie realized that, if this act were heard about at school, he would forever be branded a pervert and that his chances of dating Monica Webber would plummet from highly implausible to nonexistent. He began to fumble with his shorts since, after all, we were all standing around idiotically in our underwear. The bond of brotherhood was strong, and the peer pressure to do things together as one made the unthinkable plausible. Charlie put his hands on his hips and stared at the sand harlot on the beach.

His eyes darted back and forth between Sandy, Ted, and me. Was Charlie thinking back to the time when we spray-painted his buttocks with a peace sign one devilish night? Or was he possibly remembering when Teddy took the blame for Charlie's breaking a window of Mr. Callahan's pristine convertible during a game of street baseball? He began to fiddle with the latex waistband of his underwear and then, with the faith of a sinner about to be baptized in the river Jordon, dropped to his knees, preparing himself for the momentous event.

We were beyond the point of speaking. The only sounds were those of the incoming tide's ripple and the occasional breeze's rustling through the marsh grass as we waited for Charlie to make one of the biggest mistakes of his life.

"Come on! Do it," Ted urged.

I said nothing. I was as guilty as Ted because of what I did not do. I could easily have shouted "Stop," for the joke had gone on too long, or even coughed to make Charlie think for a moment. But I did nothing. I simply stood there and watched as my friend prepared to do something I would never do.

Just as Charlie was peeling off his underwear, a bell mercifully sounded. Most of us except for Ted had a bell that our parents would ring to call us home. I knew the chime of my summons was like no other in the neighborhood. The Smiths' bell had a low resonance, and the Millers' was more of a gong sound. However, my bell was unmistakable in its nautical tenor, and when it rang it was time for me to head home.

There was no need for explanations to say goodbye because both Ted and Charlie heard my bell as well. They knew that the sound was my invisible tether that delimited my range of exploration. On a good day, if the conditions were right, I could hear my bell from over three miles away. I turned and began to walk back to the water.

"Hey, where are you going?" Ted demanded.

"Home," I replied, barely noticing that Charlie was by my side as we waded into the creek.

"Yeah, we're going home," Charlie chorused.

Teddy was left alone with Sandy watching us depart. "You guys can't go," he said. "What about the club?"

When I reached the other side of the channel, the tide was flowing back into the creek, and the sandbar was beginning to vanish under the influx of Long Island Sound. "We can do it some other time," I shouted. "Want to come over to my house for some breakfast?"

"I don't know," Ted answered.

"I'd bet my Mom will have some sausages, French toast, and orange juice."

When Charlie and I got to our campsite, we began to retrieve our stuff, which mainly consisted of sleeping bags and matches. By the time we looked back at Ted, the sandbar had all but vanished under the rising tide, and the only feature left of Sandy was her oversized breasts defying the swelling waters.

"Hey," shouted Teddy. "Anybody seen Mixer?"

Mixer was Ted's constant companion, a good-hearted mongrel that seemed to be part Labrador retriever, part beagle, and a dash of terrier thrown in for good measure. When it came to people, Mixer did not have a mean bone in his body, despite his forbidding fangs. His fur was chocolaty with little flecks of black, a combination that camouflaged him perfectly against the backdrop of leaf litter.

Mixer knew a multitude of tricks and would wander the neighborhood shaking hands, rolling over, playing dead, and saying his prayers while begging for leftovers all over town. He never went hungry and always found his way home. When Teddy found himself in trouble or wandering alone, Mixer was always waiting to escort him home.

When Ted whistled, Mixer bounded out of the woods and splashed toward his companion. That was good because now Ted would not be alone, and it was good because it would force Ted to go either home or to his grandpa's shack. Had it not been for his dog, I think Teddy might never go home, especially when the weather was warm.

"You sure that, you don't want some eats over at my house?" I asked.

Ted and Mixer were now swimming away from what was left of the sandbar. Upon reaching the shore he immediately threw a piece of driftwood into the water for Mixer to fetch. Teddy was about to pursue his next adventure and wasn't hungry enough to waste his time on eating.

"Not hungry right now," he shouted. "I'll see you later."

"Okay, see ya."

As Charlie and I headed for home, I took one last glance at Ted. He was enthralled with his new project of throwing sticks into the water for his dog to fetch. He didn't have to go home, and I felt a bit envious of his freedom, just as I am sure he felt slightly envious of my domestication.

So for the time being our clan was split, but we all knew that eventually we would end up back together again. There would be a baseball game, or one of us would go back to the creek and hunt for arrowheads, but meanwhile for Charlie and me it was back to civilization in the form of home. For Ted, well, only he and Mixer knew where they were going, and perhaps that was for the best.

III

As Charlie and I walked up the worn path through the woods toward my home, we were both relieved by and exhausted from our unconsummated sexual experience in the sand. Even after our swim we still smelled of smoke, and after discussing topics ranging from nuclear annihilation to girls' breasts and rear ends to the space program and Mickey Mantle's knee injuries, we were all talked out.

One of the greatest advantages of our clan was the fact that we could migrate from the Neolithic age into the twentieth century in the time it took to walk the forested path leading from the woods to my home. My house had the distinction of still being surrounded by hardwood forest. No streetlights, only starlight. No neighbors except for opossums, raccoons, and deer. No horns or engines blaring, just cicadas in the summer, crickets in the fall, wind in the winter, and the returning songbirds of spring. The infestations of human beings had not come to this place, which was an unspoiled sanctuary for a young man to explore.

As we approached my two-story colonial home, the sweet smell of fried bacon and eggs wafted into the air. Charlie and I were famished. My mother barely looked up from the stove. "You boys hungry?" she asked.

We grunted in unison, "Yes," before digging into our food without saying a word, washing it down with a cold glass of whole milk.

"Where's Teddy?" my mother asked.

Charlie's food-muffled answer was barely audible. "Didn't feel like coming."

"I was hoping to get a good breakfast into that boy," my mother replied.

"Not today," Charlie replied. "He and Mixer just headed off to home."

"You're not too talkative today, Bub," she said to me.

"Bub" was a Bonacker term that people from eastern Long Island used to call each other. Bonackers were folks who made their living from the sea by harvesting clams, scallops, eels, and stripers from the natural bounty of Long Island's 100-mile-long thrust into the Atlantic Ocean. Mother's people were all Bonackers. Her family didn't have much money, but they never went to bed hungry, because they had learned how to subsist on what the sea provided.

My mother had the figure of a woman much younger than her age. She liked to smoke cigarettes and entertained herself by playing bridge with local women in the community. She also sewed much of her own clothing, even though she could afford to buy dresses at the store. Her face and hands told the story of a childhood out in the sun, helping her family dig for clams on the flats or sitting by the ocean as she watched the men fish. She never wore much makeup, and her shoulder-length brunette hair was always neatly combed.

A devout Episcopalian, she always trusted that God would protect me and my younger sister Gwen. She was strong in a demure way. Had she gone to college, I'm sure that she would have become a teacher or excelled in some comparable profession.

My mother was one of the few adults who worried about Teddy. The only other person was his grandfather, but most people around town considered the old man to be crazy because he lived a hermit's life in a two-bedroom shack in the middle of the woods. There were many rumors about that dilapidated cabin, and most people, except for the census man and Ted, rarely visited the place.

"You boys have fun camping?" my mother asked.

"Yeah," I replied.

"Do anything interesting?" she persisted.

"Just the normal stuff." My thoughts immediately ran to the sand girl.

"You mean you boys sat around the campfire and roasted marshmallows?"

"Yeah." I winked at Charlie because the only thing we roasted was a can of bug repellent that had exploded in a cloud of noxious fumes and tin shrapnel. Of course my mother didn't need to know about that detail of our campout so long as no one got hurt.

"So did you boys have fun out there?"

"Yup," we answered in unison.

"Well, that's good," she replied.

Seeing that she was stuck in a monosyllabic conversation with both of us, she stopped asking questions and retrieved our empty dishes from the table. By the sink, gazing out on our back yard, I guessed that she was thinking about her husband and wishing he was home. It was great being an airline pilot's wife, but the long separations were sometimes hard to take.

For some reason it occurred to me just then that it isn't always dramatic events that shape our future lives. A car accident, a fall through the ice, or meeting a soul mate can forever alter the course of our existence. I wasn't with Teddy when he decided to go to his grandfather's house after the campout, nor do I have any firsthand recollection of this pivotal moment in time that would eventually influence my life. I only know what Teddy told me, but that was enough to change my life forever.

I V

Between where the town started and the creek ended stood the shack of Nathaniel Wells. By all accounts Mr. Wells was not a nice man at all, and most people did not take the time or make the effort to visit him. It was variously rumored that old Nat had killed a man, that he was a shotgun-toting millionaire, and that he was a Communist spy. These reports had succeeded in keeping everyone away from him. Such whispered gossip can be a powerful thing in small towns.

Teddy's peregrinations always seemed to end up at his grandpa's house, which was not an easy place to reach. The house itself was in desperate need of repair. Its shingles, those that were left, were grey with age and enveloped by green moss. The roof, made of cedar shakes coated in creosote tar, was slowly collapsing. Moreover, the driveway that led up to Grandpa Nat's home was more dirt than roadbed. Two half-mile ruts in the ground had been gouged by a faded black 1951 Ford that the eccentric hermit routinely and aimlessly drove around town every Thursday.

According to Teddy, the unique thing about his grandfather's place was the fact that it still had a working outhouse. Old Nat had long ago upgraded to indoor plumbing, but bowel functions were still reserved for the outside stroll to what Nathaniel referred to as his honey booth.

Town authorities had asked Nathaniel Wells to annihilate this outdoor lavatory, but just as he did with every other governmental request Nat steadfastly refused. As a matter of fact, he often used these notices as reading material in his back-yard commode or as emergency toilet paper if the need arose. "Waste not, want not" was Nathaniel's favorite catchphrase for all aspects of his life.

Everything from damaged canned goods to Army surplus clothing and road kill was subsumed under that heading. Old Nat just couldn't stomach throwing things out that, given his frugality, retained some faint hint of usefulness. The life of a product, any product, took on multiple uses even after its primary function had been met.

For example, Nathaniel's Sunday shirt, after years of being starched and pressed, would eventually become sleepwear. After keeping him warm in the winter or cool in the summer, the garment would go through another metamorphosis, evolving into a work shirt to wear around town when he was looking for other recyclable items.

When the item became too ripped or devoid of buttons, it was transformed once again into squares of cloth for napkins before its final use in the outhouse. "Waste not, want not" was Nathaniel Wells's pronouncement on and response to the bane of profligate consumerism.

The outhouse behind his house remained intact no matter what the town requested or ordered. No local official ever came to knock it down. Perhaps no civic employee thought it was worth his life to tell old Nat Wells to demolish his little outhouse. Rumors had their advantages.

Ted walked up to his grandfather's house with little regard for the rumors. He and Mixer strolled past all the junked cars and boats in the yard, passed through the unlocked doorway, and settled into the kitchen. A half-eaten TV dinner rested near the sink. At this stage in his life Nat's entire caloric intake was provided by the modern wonder of processed food. Every meal was taken from his freezer, heated in his oven, and its aluminum container saved to be recycled at some later date. Nat was particularly fond of the fried-chicken entree, which also included mushy corn, salty mashed potatoes, and a brick of peach cobbler for dessert. The old man would consume this same dinner for weeks on end.

Teddy grabbed some hard candy from a dish and opened the refrigerator for a can of pop. The fridge was mostly filled with cheap beer, but there was always some soda for Ted to drink. Grandpa's house was his true home: he felt totally at ease in the clutter, and when he entered the domicile he passed into a portal of the past.

His grandfather represented a life begun at the turn of the century before the invention of cars and airplanes and when the horse was a common form of transportation. Nat had been a willing participant in World War I, supposedly the war to end all wars. Nearly blinded in a mustard-gas attack, he found out that any war is nothing more than a convoluted lie. In the muddy, rat-infested trenches outside Paris, Nathaniel Wells killed another human being for God and country.

After that Nat came home and watched the roaring twenties devolve into the bust of the thirties. Being a carpenter was tough back then, especially when nothing was being built. With a new wife and baby, Nat had to travel miles from home to work. There were weeks when he had to scratch out a living with jobs that had nothing to do with his trade.

He often found himself working far away from home. His local bank had gone under, and from then on he didn't trust an institution based on greed and lending. So he kept his hard-earned money at home, hidden somewhere that only he and God knew about. Rumor had it that Nat was a millionaire. Not really: he just saved more than he spent, and over seventy-five years that can add up.

Nathaniel Wells didn't trust most people or the banks, and most of all he didn't trust the government. In the 1960s, if a person said unfavorable things about the U.S. government and lived alone in the woods, he had to be a Red. In point of fact, Nat didn't like the Soviets any more than he liked the USA. It didn't matter whether a government claimed to be communist, socialist, fascist, or democratic in orientation. They were all bullshit to him. So whether he liked it or not, at least to the folks around town, Nat figured in the paranoia of the time as a Commie.

As Ted entered the cramped den of a house, the old man was stretched out on the putrid green couch watching a ball game. The room smelled of stale cigarette smoke and old man sweat. The couch was weary worn putrid green color, and Nat had been lying in it for so long, there was an indentation of his body dented in the cushions and springs of the sofa. Nathaniel Wells was bald and had spotted skin. His belly was potted from too much beer, which made his suspenders all the more pronounced. Even an adolescent boy could detect that this man was played out.

Nonetheless, no matter how cantankerous or tired Grandpa Nat was, this was the last safe place on the planet where Ted could go. In this house he wasn't going to get yelled at or made fun of, and he was sure to get some food in his stomach, even if was greasy fried chicken and hard candy. Teddy plopped into the only other piece of furniture in the room, a large aquamarine chair that swallowed him up in its arms and sagging cushions. As on most other days, Nat was absorbed with watching a ball game on his black-and-white television set.

The TV had a crooked wire hanger with tin foil, fashioned from a TV-dinner container, which sufficed as an antenna. The picture was always slightly snowy, and at times the device was more radio than television, but Nat still marveled at the technology.

"Hi Grandpa," Teddy yelled.

"Saint Louis stinks!" replied Nathaniel.

"Then why do you watch them?"

"Because they stink! Want some candy?"

"Nope."

"How about him?" Mixer sniffed the air and ignored the chocolate in favor of some fried chicken that was sure to come his way.

"Not today."

Nat stared at the television as the haze of interference clouded the screen. Teddy strained to see the picture, trying to decipher the players as the figures danced around the box.

"The game's not on till later today," said the old man, "but I'm trying to get a picture before the next game of the series starts. Boy, those Negroes sure can play. Ever since they let them play with the white boys, there just seem to be more and more of them playing ball."

Teddy leaned toward the television to see whether he could tell the difference between the figures on the replay of the past game. "They all look the same to me, Grandpa."

"No, if you tilt your head a bit you can see the darker ones are Negroes and the lighter ones white boys."

"If you say so," Teddy replied.

"Sure I says so. Hey, did I ever tell you how to fight a Negro?" Nat queried.

"Why would I ever want to get into a fight with a black boy?" Ted asked.

"You have to kick them in the shins. Don't ever hit them in the head. They got hard heads, and you'll break your hand. You have to kick them in the shins. You got that, boy?"

"Got it, Grandpa."

Even Teddy knew that, when his grandfather said things like this, they were wrong. Teddy didn't know any black people, and he didn't know any Hispanics, Jews, or Orientals either. He had watched as Detroit burned, fueled by race riots, on the evening news. He lived in a white suburban world where if you weren't careful you believed what people like Grandpa said about other folks. As Teddy strained to watch the TV, he wondered what black grandfathers were telling their grandchildren about him.

They both continued to stare at the screen as the Saint Louis Cardinals got ready to play another game against the Detroit Tigers in the World Series.

"They got no pitching, they got no fielding, and they sure as hell got no hitting. Detroit is just going to kill them, just kill them. Saint Louis hasn't been no good ever since the Gashouse Gang in 34 when they had Dizzy Dean. Want something to eat?" Nat slowly rose from the couch and flicked off the television, not waiting for Ted's reply, before heading into the kitchen.

It was only 10:30, a.m. but Nat was ready for lunch and more importantly his first beer of the day. Of course, at his age he usually got up at 4:00 in the morning and rarely went back to sleep. Mixer began to wag his tail, knowing it was time to beg for a meal, and obediently followed the old man into the kitchen.

Nat slapped two plates upon the table. He then brought out two empty juice jars that would serve as glasses for a can of generic Cola and a bottle of Kleinhauser beer. The latter had the distinction of being the "World-Famous Earl of Beers, a brew that won't cost a king's ransom to drink!" Nat liked the taste, but what he liked more was that a six-pack cost less than a dollar a day to drink.

The old man opened the freezer, took out three dinners, and slid them into the oven. It was a familiar routine, one they had done thousands of times ever since Ted started going to his grandfather's house. Nathaniel coughed as he sat down at the table and lit a cigarette to wait the customary twenty minutes for the meals to cook. Teddy liked this time because they could talk to each other without interruption. Of course, it was mostly Nat who recounted stories that he had told thousands of times to his grandson. With age the horrors of youth generally vanish, and the past evolves into idealized memories.

Normally Nathaniel eyes shone as he recited stories about life before automobiles and airplanes, or animated tales of playing minor-league baseball for the Brooklyn Bushwicks. Today was a little different. Nat poured his beer a little more slowly than usual, and he looked deeply into Teddy's eyes when he told this particular story. This was the first time the boy had ever heard about these events, and Nat's intensity indicated that he wanted his grandson to remember this particular conversation. It was a tale of a life-changing event buried deep in purposeful silence, one that was not to be shared with those outside the family.

After taking a long sip of his beer and wiping the back of his hand across his lips, Nathaniel leaned into the table and started talking. This time it was not his usual repertoire of recounting an acquaintance who had died or a fond memory of the past.

"My chest has been bothering me lately," he confided.

"Did you eat too much sauerkraut with your hot dog?" Teddy replied.

"No, it's not the hot dogs this time."

"Maybe you strained yourself."

"No, it's not a strain."

"So what can it be, Grandpa?"

"My ticker isn't what it used to be. That's what happens when you get old, but you have to promise me, Teddy, that you're not going to tell this to nobody."

"I promise, Grandpa."

"Did I ever tell you about the time I got into a bit of fun with your Uncle Frank? You didn't know your Uncle Frank. He died too young, which was a damn shame. We were broke; the Depression was coming on strong; and Grandma and I had just brought your Mom into this world. We didn't have two pennies to rub together."

Nat took another sip of Kleinhauser and seemed to start all over again, trying to find the courage and the words to talk about a difficult subject. He couldn't tell Muriel, his only daughter, because of her bad decisions since her husband had vanished into the jungles and rice paddies of Vietnam, and Nat didn't trust the preacher man. Inveterately skeptical about all religion, he wondered how his daughter had managed to find a character like Caleb Lovejoy in the first place. It was her life, of course, but Nat never had any use for Mr. Lovejoy. Something about him just wasn't right. That was why he couldn't tell his only daughter about his stash.

"You see," he began, "your Uncle Frank and I were helping to build a hotel out in Montauk because that was the only place we could get work. We slept in our car at night and worked during the day. I'm surprised the foreman even hired your Uncle Frank because he wasn't much of a carpenter, but no one else apparently was willing to work all the way out at Montauk. That place was the end of the Earth, and the hotel had to get built. They were going to make Montauk the next Atlantic City, you know, but that was before the Depression hit.

"So one night your uncle and I decided to go into town, which was where we met a guy who said he had come out to Montauk to do a little sword fishing. He asked us if we wanted to make some easy money for a night's work. Funny thing was that this fellow didn't look much like a fisherman, all dressed up as he was in a clean white suit, but your Uncle Frank and I didn't have no dough, so we figured what the hell. What did we have to lose? I knew something wasn't right about the situation, but money was money."

The old man took another swallow of beer, paused for a moment, and poured some into Teddy's glass. Nat had been giving a little sip to Teddy ever since the boy could walk since; after all, the old man never liked to drink alone and beer was food. Teddy grimaced at the bitter flavor, his palate not yet having acquired a taste for beer.

"So we agreed to meet down at the dock the following night to go on Mr. White Suit's fishing trip."

"What kind of fish did you catch?" inquired Teddy.

"Money fish!" his grandfather replied.

"Money fish?"

"They ever teach you about Prohibition in school?"

"Nope. Never heard of it."

"Well sir, that was another bad idea the government came up with to make sure nobody in the US of A could ever get a drink again."

Anger flared in Nat's eyes as he slammed his fist on the table with so much force that the dishes rattled.

"Oh, it's okay for me to get gassed in the trenches, it's okay for me to kill another man for my country, but heaven forbid I should want a beer with my meal! That's the thanks you get from Uncle Sam. 'Welcome back, boys. Thanks for all your help. Now enjoy some milk with dinner.'"

"What about the Money fish?" Teddy interrupted.

Nat inhaled deeply and returned to his story. "Well, it turned out that Mr. White Suit's real name was Sonny the Suit Faltucci, a Mafia hit man, and he wasn't going fishing at all. So what do you think he wanted to do with that boat in the middle of the night?"

"Hunt for buried treasure?" Teddy whispered.

"In a way. He wanted to take his boat out and meet up with some ships to transfer their English booze to us. If you couldn't make it, some enterprising lads from Limey Land were more than happy to accommodate the demand. So your Uncle Frank and I started running hooch in the Atlantic off Montauk with Mr. White Suit. We hauled crates at night from English cruise ships and made more money in a couple of hours than we could in a month for pounding nails."

"Grandpa, wasn't that against the law?"

"Law shmaw! It was the God Damn Depression! A man's got to do what a man has to do, you know what I mean? God put booze on the planet so we could drink it! So after six months of hauling hooch your uncle and I decided to expand the operation with Mr. White Suit and get a bigger boat. We started rolling in dough, but the problem was that we couldn't spend too much because, when a carpenter flips around thousands of greenbacks, that's when you start to get into trouble. Now we faced another problem: your uncle and I had all this moola but no place to put it."

"What about a bank?" Teddy asked.

"Banks! Don't you know nothing? Never trust no bank. They take your money, and when you want it back, they close up shop.

Take all your money—that's what they do. Don't never trust no bank! Besides, everyone knows that cash is king."

The old man poured out the rest of his beer and gulped it down to calm his nerves, expelling the excess gas into the air with a satisfying belch. He then got up from his chair and pulled another Kleinhauser from the yellowed refrigerator, setting it carefully on the kitchen table. The heat from the oven filled the room as he checked the progress of his dinners. Gently lifting the aluminum foil, he probed with his rusted pocket knife, concluding that the meals were still slightly frozen, and returned to the table to continue his story.

"Here's your Uncle Frank and me making dough hand over fist, and we decided that we didn't need no Sonny to help us pick up the booze. Now knowing how the operation worked, we bought ourselves a boat. Regular businessmen we were—it's the American way. The problem was that Mr. Faltucci caught wind of our plan and decided that your uncle and me were horning in on his turf. Once too many people know about something, you know it's time to get out."

"So what happened, Grandpa?"

"Well, it was the first night of our business, November 6, 1932. The water was still warm from summer, and it was a clear, calm night—no full moon, which was good because we wouldn't be easy to spot, just millions of stars shimmering in the sky. We met up with our ship, paid them off with some of our cash, and made the biggest haul to date. Of course, Sonny had learned about what we were doing. So when we were making the drop-off at Morning Dove Cove, who pops out from around the point but the Coast Guard.

"Your uncle grabbed the bottles of hooch and started to throw the stuff overboard while we tried to make our getaway.

When we were a good two miles, the God damn Coast Guard cutter fired a warning shot across our bow. We were in a tight spot, but we decided to keep going to get close enough to shore so that we could swim to the beach if necessary. It was dark, and we were pushing the boat to the limit, so when we hit some rocks we decided to swim for shore rather than face the Coast Guard. It was a good thing we did, too, because if we had stayed with the boat I wouldn't be here telling you this story. God damn government! Next shot they fired blew our brand-new boat to smithereens.

"After that experience Uncle Frank and I decided to take our cash and get the hell out of Montauk. The next morning we split up and headed back to Sayville, swearing to God that if we got out of this scrape we'd divide the money and never do nothing like this again. So when we got to the beach all wet and tired, and nearly drowned, Frank and I pledged to never speak of our rum-running days again. Me, I think that bastard Sonny the Suit tipped off the Coast Guard and paid them to blow up our boat, but that bastard eventually got his."

"What happened to him?" Teddy inquired.

"I heard he died with an ice pick through his eye. Things got a way of working out when you're dealing with clap money. That's what Frankie and me used to call the dough, clap money—easy to get and hard as hell to get rid of. Money ain't worth a shit!"

The old man took a deep breath and sat silent for a moment before finishing off his train of thought with a large gulp of his second beer. He then opened the oven again, grabbed some stained towels, and pulled the trays out to set on the table. The smell of processed fried chicken filled the room. Suddenly Mixer appeared next to Nat, drooling in anticipation of his meal.

"Gotta let it cool down before I give it to old Mixie. Don't what him to burn his mouth," Nat chuckled.

"So where's the money now, Grandpa?"

"I'll tell you one thing, boy. It ain't in no bank! Here, Teddy. Eat your food."

Being ever frugal, Nat not only read his morning paper but also used the previous day's installment as a biodegradable place-mat for his meals. Teddy thus could read the headlines while eating. He searched out areas of interest to him, which were limited to the sports page or news about the space program.

"See, Grandpa. The paper says they're building some more LEMs to land on the moon."

LEM, which stood for Lunar Excursion Module, was the craft that was going to land on the moon. Grumman Aerospace had been awarded the contract to build this unique vehicle. There always seemed to be a story about it in the daily paper, news about cost overruns or the new technology used to build it, but it was an honest-to-God spaceship being built right in Teddy's back yard.

"Look, Grandpa. Here's the aircraft that's going to land on the moon, and it's being constructed right here on Long Island at Grumman Aerospace in Bethpage!"

Nat shoveled food into his mouth as he eyed the paper that Teddy proudly shoved toward him. "That don't look like no plane to me," he grumbled. "It's got no wings and looks more like a bug than a plane. How the hell are they going to fly that thing to the moon and back?"

"They just have to get it to the moon. Once it's there, they're going to leave it up on the moon."

Old Nat's face scowled up as he forked some mash into his toothless mouth. "Now if that just ain't a Damn waste! Spending billions of dollars on a plane that don't have no wings, and they're only going to leave it up on the moon. Our government beats all when it comes to spending taxpayer money, especially on a plane that looks like a big potato bug."

"How far is Bethpage from us, Grandpa?"

"Not too far, about thirty or forty miles as the crow flies."

This was another thing Teddy knew his Grandpa was wrong about. He accepted that it was important for the United States to land on the moon. President Kennedy had said it wasn't going to be easy, but that was why we were going to do it. Americans had to be the first to land on the moon, not the Soviets. Teddy dreamed of space. He felt it in his bones and was drawn to the heavens by a manifest destiny that had been genetically programmed into his DNA.

Teddy had hardly started his meal when a new 1968 Buick Wildcat convertible pulled up next to his grandfather's tumble-down house. The black car glistened with its white top, chrome-plated headlights, and pointed fins on the back. The driver pulled gingerly to a stop, trying to keep the mud of Nat's driveway from splattering the automobile's finish. Mixer looked up from his dinner for a moment and issued a low growl.

Nat peeked through the window as he picked food from the remaining teeth in his mouth. "That dog you got is one good judge of character. Lovejoy just rolled in."

V

Fear and anger filled Teddy upon mention of the visitor's name. Mr. Lovejoy's oratorical skills instilled his parishioners with the fear of God. Divine inspiration had become his rationalization for every act he preformed, no matter how righteous or devious.

He always wore a suit and seemed to be more of a businessman than a preacher. Opening his car's door, Caleb Lovejoy gazed at his surroundings with an air of contempt. He took a comb from his pocket and carefully raked his slick black hair across his scalp. His gold Rolex glistened in the sunlight. He then extracted an initialed handkerchief from his breast pocket and dabbed beads of sweat from his face while glancing down at his muddied patent-leather shoes. Shaking his head, he walked into Nat's house without knocking at the front door.

Teddy didn't have the stomach to confront Reverend Lovejoy today and decided that it was better to hide behind the couch rather than face his potential stepfather. He found a corner in the room and made himself small. Having served in World War I, his grandfather, he knew, would protect him. Pressing his back against the wall, he tried to be as still as possible. He prayed to God to make him invisible so that he would not be discovered by Pastor Lovejoy. The warmth of Mixer's feet near his ankles suggested that God might be listening to him.

Nathaniel Wells did not rise from his seat as Mr. Lovejoy calmly strode into his home. "I did not invite you to come into my house," he declared.

"'He who seeks good finds goodwill (Proverbs 11:27).' Do you know why I am here, Nathaniel?"

"The whorehouse closed today?"

Caleb's eyes narrowed to slits. "Nathaniel, 'It is hard for the rich to enter the kingdom of God (Mark 10:23).' I am here to save your soul before it is too late. To give one's possessions to the Church and to Christ is one of the greatest absolutions. Your gift would most assuredly gain you a pathway to heaven's gate. Think of all of the good that gold can do when put to God's use."

"You've been coming here for the past three years," retorted Nat, "and I don't know what the hell you're talking about. And even if I did, it's more like I'm putting any money I might have to Caleb Lovejoy's use rather than God's. I have never seen a bigger racket in all my days. You don't pay taxes, and I never have seen a church go out of business. As a matter of fact, some of the richest clubs in the world are churches. Protestants, Catholics, Jews, Muslims, Buddhists—they've all got bigger buildings for people to visit than I do. I think I'll stick with Nathaniel Wells's invisible wizard in the sky, thank you very much. Are you telling me that all I have to do is to pay you off to move through the tollbooth of eternal life? At my age I think I'll find a back road without tolls to meet my Maker."

The preacher began to play with the utensils on the table, taking particular interest in the knives. Dangling one in his fingers, he said: "'If anyone loves me, he will obey my teaching. My Father will love him, and we will come to him and make our home with him. He who does not love me will not obey my teaching (John 14:20).'" Without warning, he slammed the knife into the table, causing the dishes to rattle and forcing a jar to shatter as it fell to the floor.

"Why must you always be so difficult?" continued Lovejoy. "God knows I've tried to be compassionate. I pray for your soul every day. I pray to the Lord to show this sinner the way to the light of eternal salvation, but Satan rules this house!"

As the self-serving preacher bowed his head to pray, he noticed that the table was not set for one person. "Nathaniel," he said, "I see that you have company."

"I was feeling more hungry than usual and decided to make some extra food."

The pastor leaned down to look under the table and noticed another tray on the floor. "Odd," he said, "that you would be eating on the floor. Only one of God's creatures would be eating there."

"The tray fell off the table," replied Nat, "and I didn't feel like picking it up."

As he listened, Teddy crouched further down to the floor, trying to become as inconspicuous as possible. He imagined himself a distant star, just a small twinkle of light hidden among the billions of other suns in the heavens. With so many stars amid the incalculable reaches of space, surely he could disappear. He pulled Mixer closer to him to feel the dog's warmth. He could smell the wet dog's musty scent, but at least he was not alone. He shut his eyes tight, praying to God to make him invisible, but as Caleb Lovejoy's footsteps got closer he had a feeling that God was too busy to listen to his prayers.

"Well, well, look what we have here. One of God's lambs has gone astray and found itself in the wolf's den. Now, Theodore, how many times have I told you not to come to this wicked place? I will not be mocked by you, boy!"

"I'm not your lamb," retorted Teddy, "and I'll go to my grand-father's whenever I want!" His muscles tensed in anticipation of the blow that was sure to come.

When the preacher reached down to grab Teddy's arm, Mixer lunged at him but was kicked back. "That dog is a menace," shouted Lovejoy "He's going to the pound!"

"You're not going to touch him, you bastard," challenged Ted.

Preacher Caleb's slap knocked Teddy into the wall. He was immediately dazed, but the blow's long-term effect would be felt some time later when he was walking to school or running for a fly ball. He tried to fight back, a counteroffensive that made the next round of punches harder and more deliberate, but the blows were carefully placed where clothing would hide the bruises.

When Caleb was out of breath and let down his guard, Teddy sprang from his spot and grabbed the lifeless clump of hair on top of the minister's head. Miraculously the toupee found its way into the boy's fingers. The bald preacher stopped for a moment, embarrassed by his own vanity. Teddy tossed the hairpiece into a corner of the room, and Mixer immediately fetched it out of the instinct to retrieve. The bedraggled wig hung from the hound's slavering mouth as his newfound prize.

Teddy prepared for the reckoning. He was sure that this second beating was going to be severe, producing welts he would feel for weeks. He curled into a ball and covered his face, but the fists and kicks did not come. Peeking through his crossed arms, he noticed that Caleb was holding a broomstick in his hand. A wild hatred blazed in the preacher's eyes as he snapped the stick in two over his knee. Smacking the handle in his palm, he stared at Teddy with a sickening glee of retribution.

"'The fear of the Lord is the beginning of wisdom, and knowledge of the Holy One is understanding,'" the preacher quoted.

With that declamation the self-righteous Caleb Lovejoy raised his hand and prepared to deliver a beating to Teddy. A sound, however, suddenly froze the preacher in mid-motion. It was a sound that needed no explanation: the distinctive click of a well greased pump-action, twelve-gauge shotgun rhythm of greased bolt action, is familiar to even the most virginal of ears, and immediately froze the preacher in mid-motion.

"The only thing you should be afraid of is the buckshot that's about to enter your backside. You lift one more hand to that boy, and you'll be meeting your Maker for a face-to-face talk."

Old Nat was leaning against the hallway opening, the barrel of his shotgun aimed squarely at Caleb Lovejoy.

"Now get the hell out of my house!" Nat said.

Outflanked, Lovejoy stared at Teddy and then at Nat, slowly dropping his arm to his side. "I'll bide my time," he threatened. "You'll be home sooner or later, boy. As for you, old man, 'The righteous man is rescued from trouble, and it comes on the wicked instead.'" Caleb then stormed out of the house, his steps hastened by the persuasive powers of Nathaniel's shotgun.

"You did it, Grandpa! You did it! Did you see him run? Did you see that bald bastard tuck tail and run? Were you really going to shoot him?"

"And how we showed him!" Nat's brief smile yielded to an angina attack as he dropped his gun and slid to the floor. "Teddy," he urged. "My pills, you know, the ones you've gotten for me before. Get my pills. I left them in the outhouse."

"Don't worry, Grandpa. I'll get them."

Teddy, with Mixer in tow, ran as fast as he could to the little white shed that in this emergency seemed so far away from the main house. Opening the door, he spotted a worn wooden seat atop a primitive twenty-foot hole in the ground. It was not a pleasant place to be, smelling as it did of human excrement and filled with insects, spider webs, and rodents' nests. Why his grandfather had left his pills in this place was a thought that flitted through Teddy's mind as he searched the cramped chamber for a vial of pills.

When he found the plastic container of nitroglycerine on the floor, he noticed that one of the boards holding up the toilet seat was loose. Teddy knew that he should go back to his grandpa straight away, but even in this situation his curiosity got the better of him. Pushing the panel aside, he discovered a hidden shelf on which rested small steel boxes. Carefully sliding one of the boxes out from the shelf, he found it packed with money. Peering back into the space, he tried to count the number of strongboxes. Although it was dark and there wasn't much time, there seemed to be at least ten, possibly twenty, shoved into a secret compartment under the toilet seat.

Teddy spontaneously grabbed a twenty-dollar bill from the top of the pile, pushed the metal box back into the hole, and replaced the board covering the shelf. Shoving the money and vial of pills into his pocket, he ran back to the house.

The pills rattled in their canister to the rhythm of his strides. Teddy felt a slight twinge of guilt about taking the twenty-dollar bill. He was sure that his grandfather had counted the money hundreds of times and knew the exact amount in each box, but maybe, thought Teddy, he would need the money to help his grandpa. It was a good excuse. If he didn't use the money, he would be sure to tell his grandfather about it later.

Teddy bolted through the screen door, preparing to save his grandfather. Alan Shepard would have been proud of him: the first American in space would have saved his grandpa the same way.

Teddy found his grandfather lying on the floor and grimacing in pain. It was not the pain of a bellyache or the horrendous throbbing of a tooth gone bad. This was an affliction that was beyond ordinary sickness. The one place in this world where Teddy had found sanctuary in his troubled life was about to be taken from him.

He ran to Nathaniel and shouted, "Grandpa, I've got the pills!" The old man had a bluish tint around his lips, and his normally ruddy complexion was ashen. He hardly looked at Teddy, his weary eyes fixed instead on the far corner of the room.

"I'll take those pills, boy," barked Caleb Lovejoy as he emerged from the shadows. Had he come back to get Teddy or perhaps to kill the both of them? Teddy did not know how a God inspired psychopath thinks. All he knew was that the preacher was back.

Cradling the shotgun in his arms, Lovejoy methodically pumped out the shells onto the floor. His toupee hung from his pocket, and had it not been for his suit and patent-leather white shoes, Caleb could have been mistaken for someone returning from a successful varmint hunt. It was obvious that the preacher didn't need the gun.

Lovejoy knelt on the floor and calmly stared at the old man. "He needs the pills, boy. Now give them to me, or Nat is sure to meet the Lord. There's no time to delay."

Caleb was an evil man, of that there was no doubt, but he had the uncanny ability to make people trust him. The way he spoke and his body language made him so believable that even those who knew his true nature were forced to capitulate. Teddy had been fooled many times by his ruses, but surely, he thought, the preacher was telling the truth in this situation, surely he was not lying this time.

Teddy looked first at Caleb and then at his listless grandfather. Nathaniel was shaking his head no, but what did that mean? Was it signaling "Don't give the pills to Lovejoy" or "I don't want to die"? Teddy was overwhelmed by the situation and the questions racing through his mind. Maybe these were the wrong pills; maybe he would give him the wrong amount. Would he inadvertently be the cause of his grandfather's death? In the background was the incessant voice of Caleb Lovejoy: "The pills, Theodore, the pills."

Teddy reached into his pocket, pulled out the plastic vial, and reluctantly placed it in on the table in the center of the room. In the process of his doing so amid the moment's urgency, the forgotten twenty-dollar bill, which had been meticulously stacked, and successfully sequestered in the dingy dank of an outhouse for more than a quarter century, accidentally fluttered onto the floor, like a butterfly landing on a summer flower. For Caleb Lovejoy the pills suddenly lost all meaning.

VI

After sleeping overnight in the woods and finishing our breakfast, Charlie and I parted ways to be alone for a while. Charlie went back to his basement full of books, and I headed back to the creek. This time I found myself tracking, examining the various paw prints on the water's edge before the tide came in and washed them out.

I would need to know how to track in case I found the last wild place left in America. I was positive that it would be filled with bear and elk, a secret area where Indians still danced around the fire at night. It would be a place that Teddy Roosevelt would have liked to hunt and ride horses, a place he would have rescued from civilization's encroachment.

I would need to be able to tell the difference between a deer and a dog print, and I would need to be able to follow the trail of a wounded buck shot with my handcrafted bow and arrows. I would not kill game for sport but would live off the land as an integral part of the ecosystem, as a warrior who was part of nature's grand design.

On the creek's banks I found the familiar paw prints of dogs, their four toes and one large pad crisscrossing the sand in a multitude of sizes. Obviously a pack of beagles, labradors, and mutts had gone temporarily feral until empty stomachs drove them home for dinner. Then there were the little claw marks of an opossum, a primitive animal that looked more like a large rat than the last surviving marsupial left in North America. However, none of these prints were the tracks for which I was searching. I was looking for the prints of Procyon lotor.

Procyon lotor was the scientific name I had memorized when looking at "R" words in the dictionary and pausing on the entry for "raccoon." It's not that raccoons weren't common to the area. There were thousands of them, as was evident by the amount of road kill around town. I was always amazed and slightly sad when Teddy found a dead raccoon. Being opportunistic, Ted would cut the tail off the beast and display the prize on the handlebars or rear fender of his bike.

However, I found it was more fun to hunt for the tracks of animals that had paws with thumbs and fingers, marveling over the fact that raccoons seemed to survive in spite of people and could adapt to our way of life quite well. They seemed to be the missing link between people and animals, a middle stage that God had created to test our hands before he put the appendages on people.

After some searching I found the unmistakable prints, the tracks wandering in and out of the creek, disappearing under the water and then reappearing back on the beach. Following their direction, I tried to imagine what the animal was looking for in the creek. Was it coming down here to look for food in the form of clams and mussels stranded in the shallow waters of low tide, or was the raccoon just exploring his territory?

Continuing on the trail, I found something entirely different, a prize that I had not counted on discovering but that would become a trophy to add to my collection. At first it looked like any other rock, a shard of quartz at the water's edge. This find, however, had an unnatural look to it. The piece had not been rounded smooth by water but honed sharp with many fine edges that a human hand took the time to fashion.

The artifact took a certain eye to find, and after years of practice I had found quite a few of the points while exploring the woods and meadows around my creek. Most of the time a chip would turn up nothing except a fleck of quartz, but sometimes, when I was lucky, the quartz would be a scraper or, better yet, an arrowhead. On this occasion, poking my finger into the sand, what came out of the ground was a true rarity—a spearhead. The weapon was three times the size of an arrowhead and bigger than the palm of my hand.

I held it in my fingers and realized that an honest-to-God Indian could have carved this piece of stone 1,000 or 10,000 years ago. The artisan had lashed the spearhead to a carefully selected sapling and perhaps killed a deer or protected his clan from invaders with this very weapon. Perhaps, I speculated, the spearhead had been lost here during a battle, waiting for me to find it in the twentieth century so that I would realize what it was like to be an Indian standing in this same spot.

With my interest piqued, the original plan of following tracks was cast aside in favor of my new pursuit of finding ancient artifacts. I became an amateur archeologist studying tools of the past by trying to discover them hidden in the sandy deposits of time. My accidental find superseded any other activity I had planned as I searched intently for another Native American relic.

Extremely proud of my discovery, I became wholly absorbed with the quest to find another artifact. The tool was all the evidence I needed to prove my theory that a sacred Indian burial ground was hidden among the nearby oaks, and I had always known that warrior spirits walked by my side. As I searched, I deduced that the Setauket tribe must have lived near the creek's edge because there was plenty of food here.

When I paused in my search for a moment, an uncomfortable feeling came over me. It was a sixth sense of sorts, and I had learned to trust it when I was alone in the woods. The invisible eye on the back of my head told me when someone or something was watching me. The sensation made the hairs at the base of my neck stand up.

I had told only Teddy about my third eye. I also had claimed that it could make me invisible at times and that I believed it was a gift given to me by a shaman spirit of the Setauket's. Teddy, being a skeptic, never believed in my proclaimed gift and decided to put my power to the test.

Ted had challenged me to steal a prize-winning pumpkin out of Mr. Heller's garden. Mr. Heller was a nasty man whose entire life revolved around his garden and who was known for his propensity to shoot animals that invaded his vegetable patch. This feat would have been difficult at night, but Teddy had decreed that I perform my magic on a sunny afternoon. The thought of getting caught or, worse yet, killed, over a pumpkin never compelled me to accept the challenge, though I continued to profess my shamanic gift of prescience.

Turning to look behind me, I spotted Charlie walking along the shore in my direction. I didn't know how or why, but once again my paranormal third eye had worked. I wondered in passing whether the Navy or the CIA, if they ever found out about my gift, would be inclined to perform experiments on me to prove my talent. As Charlie approached, I held the prized spearhead over my head and shouted, "Hey, look what I found!"

Charlie quickened his pace, never himself having found any artifacts. A scraper could be lying right in front of him, and he routinely would overlook it. Of course, there were times when Teddy or I would trade our arrowheads just to pass a math exam that Charlie had barely studied for. Talents come in many forms, but unfortunately they can't be exchanged or traded like arrowheads. It takes time to learn a talent, and the skill lies in knowing when and where it can be put to good use.

"That one is a beauty," Charlie exclaimed.

I washed the mud and algae off the spearhead with creek water, looked at it for a moment, and then stuffed my prize into my pocket.

"So where did you find it?" Charlie asked.

"At the water's edge."

"No, I mean where exactly did you find it? Over at the water's edge by the dock or by the white sand mound?"

"I don't really remember. It was somewhere around here," I said, not wanting to reveal details concerning the find.

"How could you not remember? I know that if I found it I would remember the exact spot."

As Charlie stormed off toward the creek embankment, I relished how the spearhead weighted my pocket, causing an odd clank as the quartz rattled against the knife I always carried with me.

"Hey, look what I found!" Charlie shouted.

"Did you finally find one?" I responded.

"No, come down here. You have to see this!"

Charlie was hidden among the reeds, having wandered at least fifty yards away from me. I had observed this search scenario hundreds of times. Charlie always came up empty-handed but tried to make the best of a common rock he had found on the shore. I meandered in the direction of Charlie's voice and was amazed to find my friend's discovery.

"It's a boat!" Charlie exclaimed.

"A boat?" I questioned as I trotted toward Charlie.

One thing the clan had learned over the years, the Long Island Sound had the miraculous ability to bear gifts of the most astonishing order. Of course all the items were second hand, and in the majority of cases had been purposely discarded by folks with little respect for the environment. Generally the clan found pieces of fish nets, lobster buoys, or various forms of sun faded plastics, which had floated to shore. A boat was a highly unusual prize, and the law of the sea would surely apply to its ownership.

"I claim it!" Charlie shouted.

I walked over to inspect the craft. It was a wooden dinghy half-filled with seawater. The slats were loosely packed with flaked caulking. Wood boats are notorious for leaking water into their hulls, and this boat was no exception. It was about fifteen feet long and three-and-a-half feet wide mid-ship. Square at the stern, it lacked any identifying name. The bow had some crudely scrawled numbers, but they were difficult to decipher. It was a sad-looking vessel with questionable seaworthiness, which made it a perfect find for us.

"If you want it, you can have it," I nonchalantly muttered.

Charlie's elation was quashed by his having no trailer to tow the boat home. And even if he were able to get the boat home, his parents would never let him keep it. The quagmire resulted in our clan's provisional ownership until the rightful owner surfaced or the sea reclaimed its booty.

I found an empty Clorox bottle on the beach, quickly cut out the bottom with my pocketknife and began to bail the water out of the boat. Charlie took the rudder, sail, and dagger board out of the craft to inspect them. The sail was waterlogged and quite heavy, and this combined with the boom and main mast taxed Charlie, but eventually he managed to get all the rigging out of the boat.

"Do you think she's seaworthy?" Charlie asked.

"Well, there's only one way to find out. Get me that plank of driftwood," I said.

"What do you need that for?"

"There's no paddle in the boat. We won't get too far without a paddle."

By the time Charlie returned with the makeshift paddle, I had bailed almost all the water out of the boat. He started to walk around the craft, feeling fairly confident in the boat's seaworthiness. We then pushed the craft into the creek to test its flotation.

"Seems reliable," I prematurely proclaimed, paddling the boat into deeper water.

"I'm not so sure," Charlie muttered.

Almost instantly water began to fill the bottom of the boat.

"This boat needs a name," I declared. "What do think we should call her? How about Geronimo?"

Charlie thought for a moment, not really caring for my suggestion. "I found it," he protested. "The least you can do is to let me name it!" Charlie pondered again. "How about the Monica?"

"I don't know," I replied. "Why not the Cheyenne?"

"Enough with Indian names!" Charlie snapped. Suddenly an idea popped into his head. "The Intrepid!" he shouted. "That's it, the perfect name!"

I started to repeat the name, slowly and softly at first but louder each time, until we both were shouting it in unison at the top of our lungs.

"So what do you think?" Charlie asked.

"I absolutely love it. It's the perfect name for our boat. Except there's one thing."

"Yes?" Charlie replied suspiciously.

What does Intrepid mean?" I asked.

"It means being fearless, courageous, or valiant."

"Now I like the name even more," I said. "I'm sure Teddy will like it too."

Satisfied with the designation of our craft, we began to guide the Intrepid further into the creek that we knew so well. After all, we had been swimming, clamming, and fishing in every part of these waters for the past eight years.

Floating with the tide, the boat was drifting into an area known to us as the great cattail hole, which encompassed two hundred acres of marshland. Cattails love to grow in stagnant bogs. The sludge there was not the normal mud one finds after a hard rain. This was evil dark stinky mud; a swamp of sulfurous layers of rotten egg muck from decades of plant and animal decay. A mosquito-infested place, where one misstep during a game of Manhunt could result in an entire leg's being engulfed by the vacuous depth of decay, and would require assistance to release a boy from the dank bogs grasp.

There was a rumor about town that during the Revolutionary War some British soldiers had been lured into the swamp by patriot spies and that they had become forever lost in the maze of plants, their bodies never retrieved from the primeval ooze. Many local residents credited the tale, claiming to have heard the calls of spirits still wandering the marshland and desperately looking for a way out. Of course, that legend stimulated our interest in venturing into the region. Besides, it was a shortcut to town, so long as we didn't stray from the narrow trails through the maze.

If the winds were blowing in the right direction and it was cold enough to keep the bugs away, the marshland was a perfect place to play a game of Manhunt, even though we would always return home covered in the swamp's rich black muck. Of course, Manhunt was not on our minds just now. We were interested in how the Intrepid handled.

"Think we should try to put up the sail?" I asked.

Charlie began to study the sail and looked toward the Sound to determine whether the wind was strong enough to propel the boat. In autumn warm breezes were still blowing from the South, and, even though the sail was wet and heavy, it rose regally on the mast and unfurled nicely on the boom. The Intrepid began to move faster than we could paddle, and we felt elated as we powered along in silence except for the calming sound of water rushing past the hull.

While one of us continuously bailed water out of the boat, we tacked back and forth in the creek, feeling the way the craft moved and alternating on the rudder. The hours slipped quickly away as we experimented with our newfound prize. The sun was just above the trees when the familiar sound of my bell filled the air.

"I guess it's about time we pack it in," Charlie said.

At this juncture I was steering the boat and quite enjoying myself, even though I had heard my bell. I just wanted to make a perfect day last a bit longer.

"Don't you hear the bell?" Charlie asked.

Reluctantly I began to turn the craft toward shore, preferring to perform the task in silence so as to prolong the perfection as long as possible. It was then that I heard an almost imperceptible sound of animal distress.

"Do you hear that?" I said. "It sounds like Mixer barking."

After I turned the boat into the wind, we listened closely, trying to concentrate not on the bell but on Mixer's yelping. "Now do you hear it?" I repeated.

"No, not yet," Charlie whispered.

I came about and headed for the cattail hole.

"Your mom's going to get mad," Charlie lectured.

"Shut up. Do you hear it now?"

"I hear it!" Charlie replied.

It was an unusual bark and one rarely heard from a dog as calm as Mixer. I had heard this howl only once before, and that was when Teddy had fallen through the ice two winters ago. The creek had frozen sufficiently for birds and dogs to walk on its surface, but the ice wasn't thick enough to support a boy's weight. Teddy found out the hard way. I had managed to pull Teddy from the creek without falling in myself, but Mixer had barked frantically throughout the entire event until he was sure that his boy was safely on shore. This was the same yowl.

I had to make a choice—either be late in responding to the bell's summons or find out what Teddy's dog was baying about. Neither choice was a good one, but I promptly turned the Intrepid toward the barking dog in the cattail hole. He was in trouble, and it was our obligation to help, even if Mixer was only barking at a muskrat he had cornered in the marsh.

VII

Teddy watched the twenty-dollar bill float to the floor. Caleb Lovejoy's gaze immediately shifted to it. "And just where would a boy like you get such a sum of money?" the preacher asked.

The only sound in the room was Nathaniel Wells's labored and gasping breaths. Teddy knew that it would be only a matter of time before Lovejoy forced him to divulge the money's location, but meanwhile his grandfather urgently needed his help. Then, in his moment of crisis, he heard the directive that he needed to hear. From the depths of strength that a lifetime of struggle can bring about, his grandfather said: "Run!"

Teddy reached down to grab the twenty-dollar bill and ran out of his grandfather's house with all the speed he could muster, leaving Lovejoy momentarily dumbfounded. Not knowing whether that might be Grandpa Nat's last words, Teddy simply followed his instruction.

He had no plan or destination. His only objective was to escape to a safe place. He would worry about consequences later. Teddy and Mixer raced past the outhouse, through the woods, and down a path in the oak and beech forest. He didn't want to look back because he knew what was behind him, but he needed to catch his breath.

Teddy's heart sank when he saw him. Lovejoy was tracking Teddy as if the boy were his quarry on a hunt. Looking up and down, he was trailing sneaker prints on the ground while spotting glimpses of the boy's fleeing figure in the woods.

In his youth Caleb had treed many raccoons and opossums in the backcountry of South Carolina. He took pleasure in chasing the frightened creatures and wounding them once they were cornered in a tree. It was not enough for him to shoot and kill the hapless animals. He took more pleasure in injuring the beasts so that, after they fell to the ground, he could watch his dogs rip the unfortunate prey to shreds. There were many times when he didn't even bring home the meat for his family to eat. Too bad he didn't have his dogs with him today, he thought to himself.

Teddy knew that if he stayed on the trail sooner or later Lovejoy would catch him. He had to veer off the path into the thorn bushes and poison-ivy vines that blanketed the woods. Surely that would slow Lovejoy enough for him to get away, because all that mattered to him was to escape the sick preacher's clutches.

As Teddy ran, he saw what he was looking for—a rabbit tunnel or warren in the hedge that was just big enough for a dog or small boy to fit through to escape a pursuer. It had been at least two years since he had last attempted such a route, and he wasn't sure that he could squeeze into the tunnel now, but glancing over his shoulder he could see Lovejoy closing in on him.

Diving into the opening, Teddy could feel the pricks of the thorn bushes. With each wriggle on his belly through the passageway, the briars dug into his tee-shirt and jeans, holding him back from speedy progress. He also could hear Mixer whimper as the thorns dug into the dog's fur and skin. Looking ahead into the maze, Teddy saw nothing but the twists and turns of a network of tunnels that the cottontail had constructed.

Doubt about his decision began to mount, but there was no turning back: he had committed himself to this escape route. The tunnel crept around in a sweeping semicircle. Ted stopped for a moment and peered ahead of him, hoping to see the light of an opening, but the tunnel seemed only to narrow and plunge further into nowhere. He crawled for at least forty feet and then stopped. All he could hear was the sound of his own breathing and the low panting of Mixer. Perhaps Lovejoy would pass them by, he speculated, thinking that they had continued on the main trail. Deep down he wanted to move. He wanted to see what was behind the next bend, but they needed to be silent as they listened for the whereabouts of Lovejoy.

Teddy heard the pursuer coming closer to his trapped position. He waited, hoping the preacher would pass him by and continue into the woods. Heavy footsteps pounded the ground as the man passed the almost hidden opening of the tunnel. Now all they could do was to wait until dark when Teddy was sure they could elude the preacher.

Teddy put his head down to think about what he was going to do next. Should he run back to help his grandpa or should he continue on to the creek? Where could he go? Where would he sleep? Where would he find food and water? To whom could he turn for help? Most of the adults he knew couldn't stand him, and he didn't want his mother to go back to the State hospital.

Reverend Lovejoy had summarily announced to Teddy that his mother was demon-possessed and needed prayer. Because she allegedly was beyond the help that a husband could provide, he had convinced her to commit herself. Teddy's mother had been sent away for her own good, and for the convenience of the wandering eye of her preacher mentor.

Admittedly, she had a propensity for doing peculiar things, but then again Teddy's mother had always been out of the ordinary. She was singularly devoted to her cats, her son, and Jesus. Muriel would have huge mood swings, happy and normal one moment, depressed and paranoid the next. She often spoke in tongues while folding the laundry, making a meal, or attending church, which was perfectly acceptable behavior so long as she regarded herself as a vessel for the will of God. However, standing in the middle of town at 6:00 in the morning while dressed in a nightgown and trying to sell pillowcases to commuters on their way to work, was clearly not to be tolerated. It was the final straw in the haystack of problems caused by her troubled soul. So she had been sent away to quell her embarrassing behavior with the dubious help of the State.

The town, congregation, and preacher could heave a collective sigh of relief that Muriel had now become New York State's problem. Henceforth she would not jeopardize the safety of herself or others by her whimsical behavior. Her case would require drugs or electroshock to solve, and having naively giving him the power of attorney, the Reverend Caleb Lovejoy was more than happy to sign the papers required to keep his vessel of the Almighty in a catatonic state for the rest of her life.

Teddy folded his hands and began to pray. He knew that God wouldn't let anything happen to him, so he prayed to Jesus to keep Lovejoy running down the path away from Mixer and him. When he heard the footsteps return, however, his heart sank. "I know you're in there, boy," said an unmistakable voice. "I followed your tracks right back to this spot, so we can make this either easy or hard." Teddy remained silent.

Lovejoy began to wade painfully into the thorn bushes. "Come on, Theodore," he intoned. "Your Grandpa needs your help. You can't very well help him when you're hiding in the bushes." Lovejoy could see the boy's and dog's tracks as he gingerly invaded the thicket. For his part Teddy could detect each awkward step of the preacher getting closer to him, so he slowly started to crawl through the ever narrowing tunnel.

"I hear you, boy!" said Lovejoy. "'Foxes have holes, and birds of the air have nests, but the Son of Man has no place to lay his head (Mathew 8:20).' There's no hiding from me." Teddy continued to crawl as the burrow slowly curved around and the tramping of the preacher's feet got closer.

Now finding himself in the middle of the thicket, Lovejoy knew that he was close to the boy but couldn't pinpoint his exact location. Sweat pouring from his forehead, he was winded by his efforts. "Come on now," he urged, "there is plenty of money for the both of us. We can use it to keep your momma home." Teddy listened to the persuasive words for a moment. The preacher's blandishment sounded so convincing, but after a moment's reflection he rejected it.

Suddenly Mixer shot in front of Teddy, crawling on top of him and stirring the bushes in his excitement. Lovejoy was alerted to his prey's location, but he wasn't quite close enough to pounce on the ingrate child. He needed to be a few feet nearer. With every tentative stride forward he sounded a bit more soothing. "'Many are the woes of the wicked, but the Lord's unfailing love surrounds the man who trusts in him (Psalms 32:10),'" Caleb recited as he stepped toward a movement in the bushes.

When Lovejoy was satisfied by his calculated proximity, he jumped as high as he could, ignoring the pain of the thorns, and ambushed the boy with all the momentum of his 220-pound body.

He hoped to break Teddy's arm or leg and torture him to reveal the money's location, but the frustration of landing upon empty ground infuriated the preacher. "I know you're in there, boy," he hissed. "Come out, come out, wherever you are."

Ted had followed the instincts of Mixer and crawled through the rabbit tunnel around the final bend to its exit. Boy and dog found themselves back on the main trail they had been running on from the start of their escape. Teddy crouched low because he was mere feet from his pursuer.

With one errant move the mad preacher would be upon him, so he crawled silently on his belly to create the most distance between Lovejoy and himself. Mixer, meanwhile, bounded up the trail, sniffing the ground and waiting for his master to catch up. Teddy could hear Lovejoy crashing through the brush. To run from here would be risky. He needed a little more distance, perhaps fifty yards, so that he could make it to the cattail hole, but at least now he knew where he was headed. Once he got to the marsh, he knew, the preacher could not catch him.

With each passing moment his escape came closer to reality. As long as he kept hearing the thrashing in the thicket, he could make it. At forty yards Teddy stopped. The crackling of the brush had ceased. He was tempted to stand upright and see what had happened to Lovejoy, but Mixer was looking straight at him with his tail erect. It was enough of a warning.

As Teddy cautiously peeked over the brush that lined the side of the trail, he saw Lovejoy standing in the thicket motionless. It was odd, but his shoulders straightened the moment Teddy spied the man. It was as if he had been waiting for Ted to look at him so that he could pinpoint the boy's exact location. The preacher turned slowly, a crooked smile plastered on his face, and the two stared at one another in a standoff.

"It's no use, boy," threatened Lovejoy. "I've got you now. Tell me where the money is, and I'll let you go. If you don't, I'll have to beat it out of you, and I just might beat you a little too hard."

Teddy turned and ran for his life, but oddly enough Proverbs 18:10 popped into his brain due to the countless Sunday sermons he had endured. He summoned the strength to shout back to Pastor Lovejoy, "The Name of the Lord is a strong tower, and the righteous run to it and are safe!" He had no idea where the words came from, or how he remembered them, but he knew that if he could make it to the cattail hole he would be safe.

Teddy hoped that the briars would slow the preacher enough for him to disappear into the marsh. He ran as fast as he could, the air burning in his lungs, and in the distance he could see salvation. Mixer stopped at the marsh's edge, urging his master forward with sharp barks.

A forty-foot cliff impended. Usually Teddy would slowly edge his way down this escarpment between woods and marshland. The soil was loose and eroded with little cover, and in happier times navigation of the precipice was a fun adventure, but not now because Lovejoy was closing in on him with each second he delayed. By the time Ted got to the bottom, he saw the preacher's sweaty face over the top of the overhang.

Lovejoy's normally spotless suit was torn and soiled. His face was scratched on the side with red trickles of blood trailing down his brow. Out of breath but confident of capturing the boy, Lovejoy laughed ominously. "It's no use, son. I've got you now. There's no place left to hide. You know the first thing I'm going to do when I get you? I'm going to kill that dog of yours. He was always a bother to me."

Teddy ran into the swamp and tried to stay on the paths that meandered aimlessly throughout it. He heard the loud thump of

Lovejoy's body as he jumped off the embankment at the swamp's edge. Ted had only a five- or six-foot lead on the man, and with a monumental effort of athleticism that surprised even Teddy, the preacher leaped through the cattails and grabbed Teddy's leg. "It's all over boy," he whispered.

Sensing the trouble his master was in, Mixer chomped down as hard as he could on the preacher's wrist. It was more surprise than pain that made Lovejoy loosen his grip just enough for Teddy to slip away. Teddy was exhausted and out of tricks; he didn't know how much longer he could evade his pursuer.

As Ted backed away, the reeds seemed to prop him up, making escape impossible. The preacher knew that he finally had the boy and contemplated the best way to torture Ted. His eyes were immediately drawn to the dog. Reaching into his coat, he drew out a knife.

Teddy had seen Lovejoy use the tool a countless number of times when he peeled an apple or pear. Caleb would meticulously slice the skin from the fruit and then cut the snack into neat chunks, using the blade to place them into his mouth. He now opened the pocketknife slowly so that Teddy could see the shimmer of its four-inch blade.

Tucking the weapon behind his back, he retreated slightly and began to speak in a calm tone. Lovejoy focused all of his attention on the dog, ignoring Teddy for the time being, and whistled to attract the hound's attention. "Come on, boy," he coaxed. "That's a good dog. Now come over to me."

Most dogs, and Mixer in particular, are forgiving animals. They live their lives in the moment, forgetting wicked memories within seconds of an occurrence. This trait combined with the slightest hint of food can make a dog, even an intelligent one, vulnerable to deception.

Mixer's weakness was food, such that at the slightest chance of a handout he was usually won over. Without any sign of malice in his eyes, Lovejoy motioned with his free hand for the dog to approach him. "I've a good old chicken leg for you, puppy," he said. "Come to me now."

"Mixer, no!" Teddy shouted, as the preacher moved closer to the beast.

What Lovejoy did not comprehend, however, was the magic of the muck. When he lunged to grab Mixer, an imperceptible sinking began to engulf the unaware minister. Grasping the dog by the scruff of the neck, Lovejoy glared at Teddy as he held his knife to the dog's throat.

"I know you love this dog, boy, but I will kill him right now unless you tell me where the money is!"

"I don't know where the money is," Teddy lied.

"Enough of this foolishness!" barked Lovejoy.

As he lifted Mixer's front legs off the ground, the dog labored to breathe. "One last time," Lovejoy demanded, holding the knife to the dog's throat and flicking away tufts of fur to get at Mixer's jugular.

Teddy could see that the white of the preacher's patent-leather shoes had disappeared into the mud. "It's in the house!" he shouted.

"Where in the house, boy?"

"In the hall closet in a secret compartment," Teddy whimpered.

By this time Lovejoy had sunk at least six inches further into the ooze. The mud now surrounded his ankles.

"Mixer, get!" Teddy ordered.

The dog's lunging weight was enough to make Lovejoy lose his balance and fall face-first into the marsh. Both Teddy and Mixer knew the trail, having been on it many times before. They knew where to step and what to jump over to keep them from sinking into the hidden traps of marshland.

Teddy's only plan for himself and his dog was to flee. So run for their lives they did, hoping by a miracle of God that Caleb Lovejoy would sink forever into the swamp. Ahead of them Ted could see the creek's mouth where the reeds gave way to open water. In the distance he also could see a boat that might be an avenue of escape. As soon as Mixer got to the water's edge, he began to bark. The dog detected by scent something that Teddy didn't yet know, the identity of the sailors on that boat, and he clearly recognized his master's desperation. Their only hope was that those on board would rescue them and that they could sail away to the safety of the sea.

Part Two

VIII

Our Journey

The windborne scent of Charlie and Chris indicated to Mixer that the rest of the clan was nearby. Even though he was its lowest-ranking member, with his keen sense of smell he recognized our proximity as a hopeful sign.

It was not in Teddy's nature to call for help, but he was too terrified not to scream out. This time he didn't care whether he wasn't strong or bold. This time he didn't care whether he appeared afraid because for once in his life he was, so he desperately shouted out for help.

As the unfamiliar craft drew closer, Teddy's arm gyrations intensified. The wind pushed the Intrepid with remarkable speed, and Ted felt a huge wave of relief when he determined the identity of the captain and mate. By the grace of God, he thought, his friends had been put here to rescue him. When the boat pulled within shouting distance, Charlie moved to the craft's bow.

"So what do you think of the boat I found?" Charlie beamed.

"Get in here quick!" Teddy replied.

Chris positioned the boat broadside to the beach in an attempt to show off the beauty of their prize. Perched proudly at the tiller, he waved and shouted the same Indian greeting he always used upon meeting a member of their fraternity: "Ya-ta-hey!" When hearing the phrase, Charlie or Teddy traditionally responded in like fashion, but not on this day. Chris was close enough to see the uncharacteristic fear in Teddy's face.

"What's the matter?" Chris asked.

Teddy ran to the bow of the boat and was waist-deep in water as he tried to clamber into the Intrepid. He made numerous attempts, but the water was too deep and the gunwales too high, so he slipped back into the estuary with every attempt.

"What's the matter? Not strong enough to get into the boat?" Charlie teased.

"He's out there, and he's going to kill me!" Teddy shouted.

Teddy didn't have to say it. Chris already could feel the hairs on the back of his neck standing on end. He could sense the piercing presence of hidden eyes looking at him. Looking into the marshy border of tall grass, he saw nothing but knew that something evil lurked there.

The reason the boat had sailed so easily to shore was that the wind was at their backs, and in the commotion Chris had lost control of his craft as it was pushed shore wards. The dagger board dug into the sand, abruptly stopping further movement, and the sail lines slipped from Chris's hands as the Intrepid listed sharply. Wet and wide-eyed, Teddy flopped into the boat.

"We gotta get the hell out of here!" cried Teddy.

"What's the matter? Are you afraid of spooks?" Charlie said.

"Don't you assholes understand? He's going to kill me! Turn this damn boat around and get us out of here!"

Chris could see the uncharacteristic terror in Teddy's eyes and knew they had to reach the safety of the offshore sea.

"Who's going to kill you, Teddy?" Chris asked.

"Lovejoy."

That was all he had to say. Chris had never met the preacher man, only have seen him from afar, but he had heard enough from Teddy to avoid the man. He quickly pushed the tiller away from him, trying to get the Intrepid to come about, but the wind pushed the sailors back to shore.

"Pull the sail in tight!" Teddy shouted.

Slowly the bow of the boat started its meandering tack out to sea. Teddy trained his eyes on the marsh, looking for some telltale movement in the reeds. He knew that Lovejoy was in there, but for the time being he was safe. Finally the boat turned, wind filled the sail, and the sweet taste of freedom gave Teddy a moment of reprieve.

Wet and exhausted, he slumped limply into the boat's cavity. Lovejoy could not overtake them now; the Intrepid was too swift. Teddy now knew that there was a God and that the Almighty had put his friends in that area to save him from the malevolence of the man in the marsh.

"Wait! What about Mixer?" Charlie asked.

Teddy's heart sank. "Turn the boat around," he ordered.

"Don't worry," Chris admonished. "Mixer will be alright; he always is. He'll show up somewhere down the line. He always does."

"We can't leave him," replied Charlie.

"Do you see Lovejoy?" Teddy asked.

"I don't see anything except Mixer on that beach," Charlie said.

"He'll find his way home, Teddy," Chris rationalized. "Don't worry. He'll be fine! In a few minutes we'll be on the other side of the creek. You can stay at my house. Mixer will show up there begging for food."

"We have to get him now," answered Teddy, "because if Lovejoy finds Mixer he will hurt him. Turn the boat around."

Chris reluctantly pushed the tiller away from him, and the Intrepid came about to sail back into danger—all for a dog. He could sense unmistakably that they were being watched, but the code of friendship overruled his wariness. Then an idea suddenly came to him: "We don't have to go all the way in," he said. "All we have to do is to get close enough to the beach so that Mixer can swim to the boat. He's a good swimmer."

"Of course," echoed Charlie. "That's a brilliant idea! Mixer will swim out to us, and then we can all go safely home."

Teddy began to whistle to Mixer to get his attention as Chris sailed the Intrepid within twenty yards of the beach before the wind gently forced it to the shore. It was then that a muck-covered Lovejoy emerged from the swamp. The demonic preacher grabbed the dog by his collar, his knife balanced in the free hand and a leer distorting his lips. "It's quite simple, Theodore," boomed Lovejoy in his sermonic voice. "You must come to me; otherwise this dog will die. The choice is all yours. You have twenty seconds to respond."

"We have to go in," Charlie said.

"I don't think we should," countered Chris.

Teddy then came to the only conclusion he could: "Let's go in."

When the Intrepid's keel scraped ashore, the wind pushed the sail perpendicular to the beach, and its occupants watched from the port side of the boat. Lovejoy emerged from the fringe of cat-tails, dragging Mixer closer to the Intrepid. In a swift but practiced movement, he slit the dog's jugular vein. Mixer's death was swift. Lovejoy then shouted: "The next time I tell you to do something, you'd better do it, or you'll be the one whose neck I stick. Now come to me!" He then tossed Mixer's lifeless body onto the beach, satisfied with his control of the situation, and grabbed the boat's gunwale.

A crying Teddy shrank into a ball and began to rock back and forth in total submission to the preacher. The other boys sat in stunned disbelief, never having seen anything so loved and alive actually die before. However, it was Charlie who had the most bizarre reaction to the death. For once in his life he got angry and became enraged to the point of madness.

Charlie became a cyclone of retribution, throwing himself at Lovejoy and flailing his fists without any thought of his own self-preservation. The surprise of his attack was short-lived, however. Even though Lovejoy was temporarily caught off guard by the diminutive Charlie, it was only a matter of time before he over-powered the boy and applied a choke hold. Chris could see the fear in Charlie's eyes.

"You want me to stick your pal next?" threatened Lovejoy "Nobody will ever find his body in this swamp. He'll be the next one of you to go unless you tell me where that money is. 'Do not rebuke an older man harshly, but exhort him as if he were your father (Timothy 5:1).'"

Lovejoy brandished the blood-stained blade of his knife next to Charlie's neck and stared at Teddy for an answer. Chris was almost ready to tell the whimpering Teddy to give up. Trying to calculate what to do next, he suddenly found himself thinking, "What would Geronimo do in this situation?"

He felt the sharp cold edges of the recovered spearhead cutting into his thigh, a reminder of the weapon's ancient power. Did he have the courage to be a warrior, Chris wondered, or would he fight no more? He knew what must be done. He must fight to live. He must fight for the clan.

Lovejoy was quickly losing patience. Nothing for him equaled the rapture of death. To kill, especially the weak and unsuspecting, brought him a fulfillment unmatched by any other earthly desire. It was as though God had put him at the edge of this swamp, he thought, where the bodies could never be found again, or at least until he was far away from this place. He would deliver the souls of these boys to the Kingdom before they had been corrupted by a lifetime of sin.

"Now," said the demented man, "you don't want your friend to get hurt, do you? Just tell me where the money is, Theodore."

Teddy could only stare at the beach where Mixer's corpse lay in the tidal zone, small waves pushing the dog's body to the sea's rhythm. In the span of less than a day Lovejoy had taken from him two of the most precious beings, and in a short life filled with far too much tragedy the flame of his spirit had been quelled to an ember of despair.

In the commotion the wind had shifted, and the rising tide had pushed the boat into the shallows. The preacher was now waist-deep in water. He could feel the weight of Charlie's slight frame lifting in the buoyancy of the saltwater. Lovejoy knew that he was leaving himself in a vulnerable position, but he also knew that he had these boys at his mercy. He could feel their fear; he could sense their weakness; and his confidence rose with every weightless step toward the boat. The lure of finding the money was too great a temptation.

Chris didn't really think about what happened next. All he saw were two heads and a hand holding a knife above the surface of the water. Suddenly Lovejoy did not seem so fearsome. All he had to do was to stun Lovejoy so that Charlie could break free and get into the boat. It seemed so simple: just knock Lovejoy on the head to make him drop the knife, and they could sail away from here and go home.

Chris reached into his pocket to grasp the spearhead. It fit so easily into his hand, as if it had been made for him alone and just for this purpose. The interior of the boat being hidden from Lovejoy's view, the preacher didn't even see it coming when Chris reached over and slammed his ancient weapon into the side of Lovejoy's head.

The quartz artifact sank into Lovejoy's left temple and lodged neatly there, much to the surprise of both the warrior and his victim. Chris watched as the preacher's knife disappeared into the water and the grip on his captive loosened. The once paralyzed Charlie didn't even look back as Lovejoy's arms lifted from around him. Blood pulsed rhythmically from the preacher's cranium, and his eyes expressed a combination of anger and astonishment.

The wholly unexpected turn of events reawakened Teddy's aggressive fury. Chris had seen such anger flare in his friend before. In an instant Ted was atop the mortally wounded Lovejoy and holding his head under water as the man's hands desperately clutched at Teddy. In the beginning they seemed evenly matched, but as the man tried to surface for air he weakened. The water was too deep, the hatred too strong, and the struggle gradually diminished, as simply and matter-of-factly as a tide flowing out to sea.

IX

An exhausted Teddy released Caleb Lovejoy's body into the sea. The tormentor who had tried to replace his father, more than likely killed his grandfather, violated his mother, beaten him regularly, slit Mixer's throat, and twisted Bible verses to justify his actions was gone, and he was glad.

Charlie swam over next to Teddy, his limbs weak from the drama that had just unfolded. Events had overtaken logic, and no matter how unavoidable they were a transgression of unimaginable magnitude had spilled into their lives. Chris, his knees unsteady, stumbled slowly out of the boat, not paying attention to the Intrepid as it drifted in the tidal shallows.

On shore the boys sat soaked and silent, contemplating what they should do next. Teddy then rose and went over to Mixer's body, pulling his former companion to a drier location. Kneeling, he began to caress his dog, the only creature in his life that had shown him pure, unadulterated love.

"We've got to go to the police," Charlie eventually said.

Chris added, "I'm sure that if we explain everything they will understand."

For Teddy it was too soon to think about consequences. He could only see Mixer lying in the sand. He sat next to his dog, one hand placed upon his lost friend, trying to feel something, the warmth of his body, the heaving of his chest, the rhythm of a heartbeat. There had always been Mixer and Teddy, without one there was no other. This loss the last of many, was unendurable. The pain of it delved deep into his very soul. A part of him was gone forever.

"Maybe we should go to my parents," suggested Chris. "They will know what to do."

"We need to go to the authorities," remarked Charlie. "We're just kids. They will understand that it was a matter of life or death."

Teddy said nothing. Wading into the water, he dragged the preacher's body to shore and, summoning all his remaining strength, dumped the remains next to Mixer. Staring blankly at his two friends, he then murmured: "Before I go to prison, I want to see the spaceship. I'm going to Bethpage and Grumman Aerospace."

X

She wasn't just angry; she was mad with a mother's worry. She had rung the bell so many times, and Chris had uncharacteristically not shown up for dinner. Hours later she was retrieving the cold chicken breasts, soggy potatoes, and wilted string beans from the table. Covering over the unappetizing meal, she placed it in the refrigerator to make a casserole at a later date.

Looking out the window as autumn's darkness descended, the last of the red and orange hues of the sun's rays vanishing below the treetops, she knew that something was very wrong. Her son should have been home by now, and it was too late to send Gwen to search for her brother. She contemplated picking up the phone and calling her husband for help, but what assistance could he provide from halfway across the world?

Gwen sat at the kitchen table, neatly dressed with her brunette hair tied back in a ponytail and her books splayed open, as she wrote in a notebook. Her brother was a constant nuisance, tormenting her with dead animal parts or uninteresting conversation, and quite frankly she was relieved that he was absent for a while. She was confident that Chris would eventually come home blabbering about some preposterous story and covered in stinking mud. Her thoughts were mainly preoccupied with older boys, friends, and school. Most of all she was angry at being unable to use the phone to keep in constant contact with her girlfriends concerning current school gossip.

"Don't worry, Momma," said Gwen. "He'll be home soon. Chris always comes home late. He probably found some dead animal that was hit by a car and decided to eat it for dinner. If I were his mother, I wouldn't let him get away with being late for dinner. I'd ground him for a week."

Gwen tried to reassure her mother with humor in hopes of gaining access to the phone, but her mother was absorbed in thought and, much to her disappointment, not paying much attention to her, despite her witty comments. Gwen had learned long ago how to manipulate her father, but momma was different. Clever conversation never impressed her, least of all from her daughter.

When the phone rang, the mother flashed a stern look in Gwen's direction, and her daughter wisely knew not to protest. Lifting the receiver, Mrs. McKellar anticipated that her son would be on the other end of the line explaining that he had lost track of time and was at a friend's house. She was wrong, however. The caller was another mother with the same nervous edge in her voice. A tension preempted the usual niceties that form a preamble to telephone conversation.

"Hello, Peggy. This is Lillian. Lillian Fairchild."

Peggy was not one to socialize with Lillian. As a matter of fact, the first time Charlie ever came over to play with Chris, Lillian had to thoroughly inspect the premises before she let her son set foot in the home. Obviously they passed the test, but that was as far as further parental contact went. The Mackellar's were never going to be of the same social stratum as the Fairchild's, not at least in Lillian's estimation.

"Hello, Lillian."

"Can you tell Charles that he has to come home now? It's getting quite late, and his father and I have to go out for a dinner engagement. He should know better."

"You mean that Chris isn't at your house?"

"Why, no."

The tone of the conversation immediately changed from annoyance to worry.

"I rang the bell at least an hour ago," continued Peggy, "and there's still no sign of them. When I ring the bell, Chris usually comes right home, but not this time." Peggy took a quick drag from her cigarette.

"Ring the bell?"

"Yes, that's how I summon Chris to supper."

"Interesting." Lillian had provided Charles with a watch long ago and found the notion of bell ringing a droll concept.

"Maybe they're over at Teddy Hooker's house," Peggy speculated.

"Teddy? I've never met him. Where do they live? What does his father do?"

Trying to explain to Lillian that Teddy was a troubled but good-hearted teenager whose father had been shot down somewhere over Indochina and whose mother had not been quite the same ever since the incident would not have gone over well with Lillian Fairchild. So Peggy kept it simple.

"He's a young man they know from school. I'll call Muriel, Ted's mother, to see whether they're over at his place. Then I'll call you right back."

"I'm afraid I don't know the Hookers. That's quite an interesting name. Do you have my number?"

"Yes, it's in my book."

"I'll be waiting for your call. Charles's father and I are expecting to leave within the hour."

"Talk to you soon."

Peggy hung up the phone, feeling successful in diverting Lillian's inevitably disapproving judgment of Teddy. She would let Charlie tell his mother about Teddy when he was ready. Peggy had learned long ago to take these adolescent matters one step at a time.

Finding her address book in the kitchen drawer, she looked up the Hookers' telephone number to make the dreaded call. Muriel was an acquaintance of Peggy's, someone she would stop to speak to at the supermarket or post office. Since her husband's disappearance Muriel seemed to be in an altered state of reality, interjecting prayer into every aspect of her life. She would drone on endlessly about praying to find food in the refrigerator praying for the car to start, or praying for money. This was a difficult concept for Muriel given her practicality. God had a place in her life, but not without the hard work associated with His grace. She believed that God favored those who exerted themselves in everyday life, and she had learned to keep any miracle the Almighty might bestow upon her personal and private.

When she dialed the Hookers' number, the line was busy. Peggy didn't call Muriel often, but when she had in the past Teddy's mother always picked up the phone promptly. Peggy hung up the phone and took another drag on her cigarette.

"Momma," implored Gwen, "can I use the phone now?"

"Not right now, honey."

Peggy dialed the number again, but the line was still in use. Walking outside to the back stoop, she rang the bell in a final attempt to get her son's attention. She was hoping to see Chris, Charlie, or Teddy emerge from the woodland dusk; however, the only sounds were those of the oaks' wind-rattled branches and the maples' rustling of autumn leaves. There was still no sign of her son.

Going back to the phone, she dialed the Hookers' number a third time without success. Gwen watched her mother pace and then reach for another cigarette from her bag. It was unusual for her to smoke two in a row. Peggy dialed Muriel's number yet again with the same result. Perhaps, she thought, the phone had fallen off the hook, or perhaps the boys were using it to make prank calls. It was time to drive over to the Hooker residence.

Peggy opened her pocketbook and began to search for her car keys. She stopped for a moment, took a deep breath, and involuntarily bowed her head. Even though it was not in her nature to do so, she took a moment to ask God to make sure that her son was safe.

XI

They set sail away from the marsh after little conversation or deliberation. Teddy had dragged the two corpses into a swamp hole, first Lovejoy's and then Mixer's. He found the muddiest pit of ooze and let Lovejoy's remains sink into it. When the body had almost disappeared, he gently positioned Mixer's body next to the preacher's. He later explained that he did so in order that Mixer might stand vigil over the spirit of Lovejoy to keep him forever stuck in the hole, his evil spirit unable to torment the living ever again.

The wind was from the Northeast, and the Intrepid navigated easily westwards. Its occupants sailed past the coal-fired Northport power plant, its orange and white towers serving as an easy landmark in the fading light. Pushing onward, the boys found themselves in the midst of a fall feeding frenzy of fish.

The waters teemed with life. Acres of striped bass filled the cove, gorging on the bunker that had taken refuge in the harbor. Their quarry's oils slicked the top of the water as they were decimated by the stripers. Amid the bloodlust mayhem, bluefish torpedoed in on the prey, and chopped fish parts boiled in the deep green water.

Screaming, opportunistic seagulls dove into the waves, feeding on the wounded fish and reaping the bounty that had magically appeared below them. The flock grew as birds flew in from all directions. Soon the Intrepid was surrounded by hundreds of diving gulls and hordes of migrating stripers. The fish were fattening themselves up for winter before freezing Arctic air would overtake the Sound. The blues and stripers would then depart for warmer water, following their food supply south.

Charlie and Chris laughed uncontrollably as this seasonal wonder engulfed the Intrepid.

"I can almost touch them!" Charlie shouted.

"We can catch one!" Chris said.

"Don't put your hand in the water, or you might lose a finger!" Teddy yelled.

"Shit!" complained Chris. "We don't have any fishing gear. If I only had a goddamn fishing pole, we could be enjoying striper tonight."

Teddy rose from his seat and evaluated the water in front of him. Exhilarated by the primal urge to hunt the encircling schools, he began to punch a paddle into the boiling mass of fish, hoping to wound one so that they could pull it from the water. In all the excitement the clan had failed to see another boat approaching the Intrepid.

"Jeeeesus Christ!" cried the lone fisherman as he cast his lure into the swarming school, catching a bass with each cast with little regard for the unofficial rule of taking only what one could eat and nothing more. The boys watched as this "sportsman" landed one fish after another, all the while exclaiming at the good fortune he had stumbled upon while on his journey home.

He was a burly man with unkempt dark hair whose face was covered in a three-day stubble of beard. His belly protruded from a soiled shirt, and an ash-laden cigar dangled loosely from his lips.

Each fish that landed on his deck was followed by the clanking of beer cans drained during his idle hours of fishing. Had it not been for this accidental bonanza, he would have come home from his excursion empty-handed.

Feeding frenzies are mysterious events, appearing without warning and suddenly ending. The two boats were alone in the water once all the fish had vanished. The three boys and the man now found themselves floating on a quiet battleground.

"You didn't catch no fish?" shouted the elated man as he cranked in his line.

"Didn't have a pole," Chris answered.

As the man pulled his craft broadside to the Intrepid, his scow of a boat appeared as beat up as its occupant. "You boys from around here?" he asked.

"We're from Northport," answered Charlie. "We were just following the fish."

"It's getting dark," said the man. "You fellas better be heading home soon before night settles in. Your parents will be worrying about you."

"They know where we are," Teddy lied.

"Need a tow back to shore? You can call your folks from the marina when I pull in. Let them know you're okay. I put in just over there by the lights at Cold Spring Harbor." The man pointed to the lights half a mile in the distance.

"It wouldn't be right because we're trying to get our sailing merit badge," replied Teddy, "but thanks anyway."

"Sailing merit badge? Well, you should have brought your poles out here." The man looked down and threw one of his just caught fish into the boys' boat. "There." He said. "Take one home and start to head in. Maybe you can get your fishing merit badge too."

The man then started to chug off slowly, his craft following a course he had taken so many times before that he didn't need a compass to find his way home. Ever since he had retired from the New York City Fire Department, his days were planned around being out in his boat and his nights around drinking himself to sleep with six-packs of beer.

Carmine had no hobbies except fishing, and his pension was just enough to keep him economically comfortable. His children had all moved away from Long Island because of its high cost of living, and his wife had died of cancer two years ago. Ever since retirement he had felt guilty about not working, but he had convinced himself that he deserved the rest.

He had thought about retirement all his life, starting from the time when he delivered groceries for twenty-five cents a day to help his folks during the Depression. He had prayed to God about his retirement during D-Day when he ferried young soldiers in his Higgins boat onto the beaches at Normandy and then watched them get blown to pieces. He also had contemplated it when as a fireman he carried charred bodies from burning buildings. When his well deserved retirement finally arrived, he never looked back.

Carmine had put his three kids through college, and he and his wife were going to travel—maybe go to Hawaii or buy a condo in Fort Myers, Florida, so that they could relax together in the winter sun. He could fish off a pier and catch some snook or perhaps, if he was lucky, a tarpon, but that was before Lizzy contracted cancer. By the time they found out about it, it was too late, and his God-fearing wife, who never missed a Mass on Sunday, soon died, leaving him alone and his plans for retirement abandoned.

Somehow seeing the boys out on the Sound made Carmine feel good and gave him a bit of hope. So he would power back to the marina, fillet his fish, grill fresh striper tonight, freeze some, and give the rest to neighbors. However, before he did all that, he would make sure that little sailboat reached shore safely. He may have had a beer belly, may have been in the habit of smoking too many cigars, and may have long since stopped working for the New York City Fire Department, but he was still a fireman at heart.

XII

The freshly caught striper, its belly swollen with bunker, flopped helplessly on the Intrepid's deck. It was a beautiful fish. The creature's three-foot-long, torpedo-shaped body, bright silver and white, had distinct black lines etched along its glistening sides. A spiked dorsal fin was fanned upward, and its tail fin was supported by a muscular caudal area as thick as a man's ankle. The striper's huge mouth gaped open as the fish helplessly gasped with oxygen-depleted gills.

"Wow!" exclaimed Chris. "It looks like we're going to be eating striper tonight."

Charlie immediately dropped to his knees and began to analyze the fish. While holding the bass down, he carefully estimated its length and girth. Holding up one of the striper's translucent scales, Charlie examined it in the last dim rays of the fading light.

"You know, they say you can gauge the age of a fish by counting the lines that encircle its scales, just like the rings of a tree. You can also see that it has no visible teeth, only small ones located on the vomer plate in the roof of its mouth."

Charlie adjusted his glasses and began to insert his fingers into the creature's mouth, but he was startled when the seemingly dead fish suddenly sprang back to life. "I was going to suggest that we examine the stomach contents to see what it was eating," he commented while Chris burst out laughing.

"Don't worry," Chris said. "When I clean that fish, you can examine its guts all night long."

"Let it go," Teddy stated.

"What do you mean, let it go? Some guys fish for years and never catch one like this!" Chris exclaimed.

"I said, let it go, before it dies," Teddy whispered.

"Technically," remarked Charlie to Chris, "you didn't catch the fish. That other fellow did. He was just kind enough to give it to you."

"Put it back where it belongs, back into the sea!" Teddy ordered.

"I will not," replied Chris. "I got that fish fair and square, and I'm going to keep it!"

"It's not your fish," Teddy responded. "All of us own a piece of it."

"Normally," interjected Charlie, "I would say let's divide it into thirds, but that's quite impossible. We will have to put it up to a vote."

"We should keep it," Chris shouted, "so let's divide it up into thirds when we eat it tonight."

"Put it back now before it dies," Teddy said.

The deciding vote was Charlie's. He looked down at the struggling fish. He hated being in this position with little time to make a decision. The scientific method of making a calculated choice always worked best when there was time to do it, but not here and not now.

Before Charlie could reach a decision, Teddy grabbed the striper and thrust it back into the water. Outraged, Chris began to scuffle with Teddy on the pint-sized Intrepid.

"You can't do that!" he screamed. "Charlie didn't vote."

"There was no time," Teddy said. "The fish was going to die. It had to be put back into the water."

As the altercation escalated beyond a friendly wrestling match, Charlie rushed into the fray and grabbed Teddy's arm, which was twisted around Chris's neck. "Stop it," he shouted. "What are you trying to do, kill each other?" Charlie then splashed water on his friends just as the Intrepid beached on the shoreline.

When the craft came to a grinding halt, the altercation ended as quickly as it had begun. The land in front of them seemed to be a private beach of one of the homes in the area or perhaps of an association that had the foresight to conserve it for collective use in the heat of summer.

In the fall the beachfront was deserted, and so the clan had the seaside all to themselves. This was good because they needed to organize a campsite. There was wood to gather for a fire and a shelter to be constructed, and of course drinking water to be found.

As they dragged the Intrepid to shore, the closer they got to the beach, the heavier the craft became. It was good for Teddy and Chris to haul the boat because the task drained away some of their recent anger with each other. Conversation was kept to a minimum as the three explorers stepped onto land.

"I claim this land in the name of Queen Isabella!" Charlie shouted as he ceremoniously planted a piece of driftwood into the beachhead. It was a futile attempt to get Teddy and Chris to speak to one another as these two members of the fraternity reconnoitered their new surroundings in silence.

By now it was getting dark, and the remaining light had begun to fade below the horizon. Chris found a perfect location to bed down for the night under a massive tree that had collapsed. Its bark had long since fallen away, leaving only the smooth, salt-whitened wood. The trunk's diameter was at least three feet, which provided adequate protection from the wind, and any heat from the nearby fire would be reflected back on the campers as they rested for the night.

"Charlie, over here," Chris shouted.

"Looks good to me," said Charlie, "but I'm very thirsty and need some water."

"I see a path leading up to a road," answered Chris. "Some houses must be up there, and where there are houses there's bound to be water faucets."

"You'll need some sort of container for the water."

Both boys turned their eyes back to the beach. On all ocean shorelines and inlets is a cornucopia of discarded items that can be adapted for use: multicolored rope, lobster-pot buoys, lures, fishing line, and of course beer cans, wine bottles, and milk jugs. Even the Intrepid was a gift from the sea.

Just as Charlie and Chris were about to embark on their beachcombing quest, a strange figure emerged from the darkness. He was a Shaman, draped in canvas with empty plastic containers around his neck that clunked in hollow tones as he walked toward the campsite. Teddy dumped his booty on the ground next to the fallen tree.

"I found some cover for the night," he said. "This stuff should keep us warm, and if we need more tarp material, we can always use the Intrepid's sail."

"Where did you get all of this paraphernalia?" Charlie asked.

"There's a whole marina of junk up there, boats covered for the winter and even a working water faucet. Law of the Sea."

Teddy had to say no more. When it came to the Law of the Sea, any item found on or near the water was available for anyone's use.

"Did you see any matches in any of the boats?" Chris asked. "We need matches to start a fire."

"Nope, couldn't find any matches. It's getting pretty dark up there."

"If it were light out, we could use one of the lenses in my glasses the way Piggy did in *Lord of the Flies*," Charlie said.

"*Lord of the Flies*? Never heard of it. When did that come out in the movies?" Teddy asked.

"You know, we had to read it in Mr. Slick's English class. Don't you remember?" Charlie stated.

"Excuse me," interjected Chris. "You're talking about Teddy. He barely made it to school, much less English class, you moron. Besides, that's not going to help us without some sunlight."

"Perhaps we could start a fire by rubbing two sticks together," proposed Charlie. "After all, there were times during the dawn of mankind when no matches were available."

"Guys, I think we have company." Teddy immediately ducked behind the fallen tree, and his two blood brothers followed his lead.

The headlights of a car shone down the deserted road leading to the little marina. Once the vehicle was within the parking lot, the lights of what appeared to be a Galaxy 500 Ford LTD sedan were turned off, and the car crept to the end of the lot within twenty feet of our tree encampment. Two older high-school students of the opposite sex then parked to observe the evening stars reflected off the water.

We were close enough to hear the couple's conversation and their radio's pop music. Just before the two lovers embraced, the young man nonchalantly tossed his smoldering cigarette out the window.

There was the fire we needed. All one of us had to do was to creep up to the glowing ember and abscond with it, but the two lovers apparently were about to get down to some consensual business.

The breathing, the giggling and the low counterfeit tones of discontent commenced the dance. Chris motioned to Charlie, pointing at the cigarette butt. Teddy, being more interested in the lovers, gestured with a finger over his lips for the other clan members to remain silent, and they watched as the girl was cornered with kisses on the passenger side of the car.

"What movie should I tell my parents we went to see?" she whispered.

The young man began slowly to unbutton her blouse, meeting with little resistance from his partner.

"Tommy! Which movie, so we don't say we saw different shows?"

Tommy seemed to have little interest in the logistics of their date, being much more engrossed in the female anatomy he was fondling. As he kissed her neck, and the forbidden region of the girl's pelvis, she snapped back to the former topic.

"Which movie should I tell my mother we went to see?"

"Donna, come on! I don't know. Tell her you went to see *Dumbo*!"

"I can't tell them I went to see *Dumbo*. That movie hasn't been out in years."

"Alright, say that you went to see *Bonnie and Clyde*. Your father probably likes Faye Dunaway, and your mom probably likes Warren Beatty."

"My dad thinks they're both Communists. Besides, there's too much sex in those movies."

"How about *The Dirty Dozen*?"

"Too violent."

"Your dad has to like Ernest Borgnine or Lee Marvin. They're no Commies."

Satisfied with her alibi, Donna pulled Tommy to her, and the kissing resumed. They obviously were enthralled with each other's bodies. Their smells, tastes, and feels, of intimate regions forbidden in normal settings, became totally acceptable as they explored each other in the wonderment of first-time love. She began to moan with whispers of pleasure, as the rhythms of their encirclement pulsated with an ever increasing crescendo of pure lust. The surprised sensation of their internal warmth felt so right, as Donna murmured a hint of delight as they entered into an enthralled point of no return.

The car rocked in explosive movements of athletic proficiency, unmatched by any sprinter on their track team. The clan could feel the heat emanating from the cars steaming capsule of passion, as the two developed into one. Donna and Tommy screamed in a symphony of violent ecstasy as they both climaxed in a primal explosion of pure hormonal love lust. They were in love, a teenage obsession unmatched with its intensity and focus, oblivious to anything other than the pure satisfaction of holding each other in their arms.

Suddenly the cigarette lost its importance to the onlookers, who sat mesmerized in voyeuristic absorption. With the show temporarily over, Chris motioned to Teddy in commando fashion, pointing toward the still smoldering cigarette. This was probably not the right time to retrieve the dying ember, but unless it was acquired soon any hope for warmth during the night would be lost.

As the lovers regained their composure, Tommy's face was illuminated as he lit up another Winston. Leaning back and exhaling, he offered the smoke to Donna. "Want some?" he asked.

"No, we should be going."

"We just got here!"

"I know, but if we are lucky maybe we really can go to see a movie."

"I thought we had that all worked out."

"I think we should leave this place. Somebody could come down here and see us."

"Don't worry. We'll be safe down here. Nobody ever comes to the beach this time of year."

Before Teddy or Chris could make his move, Charlie began to crawl toward the smoldering prize. It was too late for either Chris or Teddy to take the initiative, and rather than risk exposure with three bodies crawling across the open field, they watched as their friend awkwardly made his way across the ground.

Thankfully this was not a combat mission, because if it had been Charlie surely would have been shot to pieces as he crawled crab-like on hands and knees toward his objective, with his rear end humped high in the air. This feeble attempt at stealth was negated by the scraping noises of his appendages on the ground, and the only time Charlie didn't make noise was when he didn't crawl at all.

"I hear something!" Donna whispered.

"I don't. It's probably just a possum or raccoon," Tommy scoffed.

"No, I definitely hear something. Let's leave!"

"Come on, baby. We just got here."

"Shhh, listen."

Charlie was about halfway to his objective, but Donna clearly possessed a suspicious nature. "I want to leave," she reiterated.

"Come on, Donna. It's so nice here."

"Let's go now."

"Aren't the water and stars beautiful?"

"I want to go!"

"But it's so romantic here."

"What don't you understand? Let's go now!"

"Okay. So where do you want to go?"

"The movies. Let's get out of here!"

"Alright."

With that, Tommy flipped his half-smoked cigarette out the window and fired up the engine. He then executed a donut maneuver around the parking lot, spinning his wheels as he sped off, while Donna bitched at him concerning the evening's encounter. It was clear the two were destined for a disastrous lifetime of matrimonial devastation. In his haste, however, Tommy had driven over Charlie.

Fearing the worst, Chris and Teddy ran toward their friend, who was lying face down in the gravel parking lot. Kneeling beside Charlie, Teddy slowly turned him over as a sinking feeling returned to his stomach.

"Charlie, can you hear me? Are you alright?" Chris said.

"Is he breathing?" Teddy asked.

Charlie's hand rose into the air. Clamped between his thumb and forefinger was the smoldering cigarette. Somehow he had managed not to get flattened by the wheels of the car while securing his fire starter.

"I don't know how you did it," exclaimed a beaming Teddy, "but God seems to have a way of protecting the simple-minded."

"How did you manage not to get smooshed by that car?" Chris asked.

Sitting up with his glasses askew and his body covered in dirt, Charlie provided a simple answer: "When I crawled over to get the cigarette butt, the car passed directly over me in the center. One centimeter in either direction, and I would have been injured or perhaps killed. I'm lucky to be alive."

"Luck had nothing to do with it. God was watching over you," Teddy said.

The tension of Charlie's near-demise was replaced by relief that he was alive. So were they all, at that moment, intensely alive because they were here, living life on the brink of adulthood. Though exhausted and hungry, they knew the satisfaction of shaping their own destiny, at least for the short term. Their quest was an adventure in maturation and the discovery of life.

Walking back to their campsite, the boys prepared for the coming night. Shoving the smoldering cigarette into a mound of dry grass and twigs he had constructed, Charlie blew on the glowing ember until a small spark ignited the tinder. They had a fire!

"Stay here and keep the fire going," Teddy said, "while Chris and I collect more wood."

While the pair searched for fuel in the darkness, feeling the primal comfort of the flickering campfire at their backs, Chris asked, "Why did you let my fish go?"

"It seemed the right thing to do."

"We wouldn't be hungry now if we had that striper."

"I couldn't stand to see any more dying today," Teddy confided.

Chris now understood his friend's earlier action, and further explanation was unnecessary. The incident was over and done. Their friendship was more important than the fish. It was a lesson in what takes precedence in life. They now could return to the campfire and its warmth as recommitted friends.

XIII

It was impossible for Peggy to sleep. The normal drowsiness that graced the end of each day had been replaced by a profound and disturbing anxiety. She wanted to be able to do something to look for her son, but it was better to wait by the phone to keep abreast of any news concerning Chris. She had waited over an hour after sunset for Chris to straggle home, but there was no sign of him. Her son had not returned from wherever he was, and at this point her goal was to remain calm. Peggy fought to suppress the terror that threatened to consume her every thought, imagining the worst things that could have befallen Chris—freezing to death, drowning, and kidnapping.

Turning on the early morning news for distraction, the worried mother heard a commentator reciting death counts in Viet Nam. The anchorman, with slicked-back hair and heavy dark-rimmed glasses, droned on dispassionately as he read the numbers over the air: "One hundred and sixty-two Viet Cong were killed today at a cost of thirteen American soldiers killed in action and twenty-seven U.S. troops wounded."

Peggy could have cared less about the politics of an undeclared war in this Asian country or the United States' commitment to stopping the global spread of Communism. Right now all she cared about was Chris's safety as she waited until her husband arrived home from overseas. These were the times when she relied on prayer to push the demons of doubt from her mind.

Peggy closed her eyes and began to pray. "Please, Lord, keep the boys safe. Lord, shield them from evil. Guard them from the cold and inclement weather so that they may return unhurt. Lord, give me strength and confidence in knowing that you are watching over those boys. Amen." The faith behind this communication with her Maker gave her the peace to think clearly. That was good enough for Peggy because she knew God was listening.

She started afresh with her thoughts. What did she actually know for certain? She knew that the three boys were together because of their close friendship. She also knew that the last time she had seen Chris he was on his way through the woods to the creek. The boys always met at the creek, so that would be the logical starting point for a search. The question was exactly where. She and Gwen had checked the camping sites at which the boys usually stayed, and there was no sign of them there, so they must have ventured beyond those places. But where would they go?

Just then the phone rang. Peggy quickly picked up the receiver, hoping to hear some good news.

"Hello, Mrs. McKellar. This is Detective Wainwright from the Suffolk County Police Department."

Peggy's heart sank. "Yes," she replied.

"I spoke to Mrs. Fairchild, and she said your son is missing as well. Usually we wait twenty-four hours on a case like this, but because of the boys' ages we are starting the search earlier than usual. There doesn't seem to be any sign of the boys. We have already searched the local area, and as you can imagine the Fairchild's are quite concerned about their son."

"Have you talked to Muriel Hooker yet?"

"As a matter of fact we did, but the woman is a bit overwhelmed at this point."

"I'm sure she is worried sick about Teddy."

"Yes, she is, but she also had just gotten news about her MIA husband. It seems that he escaped from a prisoner-of-war camp in Vietnam, a bit of a miracle if you ask me. She was understandably overwhelmed by the good news but not too helpful with details concerning her son. We were hoping that you could give us some information concerning the boys' last-known whereabouts. That way we can start to get our bearings concerning their possible location now. The more people we have involved in this missing-person report, the greater the probability that we will find them."

It was the first time that Peggy had heard the term "missing person" applied to one of her offspring. She choked back her emotions and became almost angry because deep in her heart she knew that Chris was many things but not a missing person. Her son knew his way home. Of that fact she was absolutely certain.

"They've found Muriel's husband," Peggy replied to Detective Wainwright. "What miraculous news! Teddy will be so happy. But now I have to try to think where the boys are. Where could they be?"

"Anything will help," said Wainwright. "What's your son's full name?"

"Christopher Thomas McKellar."

"Your address?"

"17 Sheps Creek Lane."

"Town?"

"Northern Shores"

"Your son's date of birth?"

"September 12th, 1953."

"So he's fourteen."

"Yes. He just had a birthday."

There was a pause as Detective Wainwright wrote down the preliminaries of his interview. Experience had taught him that basic information was vital when searching for missing persons.

"Can you give me a description of what your son looks like?"

"He's about five feet and nine inches tall and approximately 120 pounds when soaking wet. Light complexion, sandy brown hair."

Now that she had explained the appearance of half the children in Suffolk County, the detective needed more detail. "Does Chris have any distinguishing features?" he inquired.

"Distinguishing features?"

"Yes. For example, does he walks with a limp or have a birthmark of some sort?"

Peggy tried to think of something unique to describe her son. Suppressed emotions suddenly overwhelmed her at the realization that her son might not be coming home soon or perhaps ever again. She began to do something she rarely did—sob uncontrollably. Like a mother who doesn't have an answer to where her boy is, she thought of the infant she had once cradled in her arms. She was unable to speak.

The silence momentarily surprised the detective. It certainly wasn't something that was uncommon, but this woman sounded so strong. "Mrs. McKellar?" he prompted.

She struggled with her words. "A scar. He has a scar above his right eyebrow. He got it when he was two years old and tripped over a rug in the garage. It's about two inches long and barely noticeable to me, but I suppose it's a pronounced mark to others."

"How long do you suppose he's been gone?"

Peggy glanced at the kitchen clock; it was almost 6:30 Morning. "He left the house around 1:30 this afternoon, so he's been gone about sixteen hours."

"That's good."

"Good? What do you mean?"

"It's been less than twenty-four hours."

Peggy didn't like the tone of that response.

"Has your son been having any problems in school or at home lately? Does he take any kind of drugs that you are aware of?"

The question snapped Peggy out of her momentary daze. "Drugs? He's only fourteen years old."

"Mrs. McKellar, we live in different times—television, divorce, rock-and-roll. Children are exposed to things of which our generation had no conception. Any problems at home?"

"What do you mean?"

"Problems between you and your husband might lead your son to run away."

"Absolutely not!"

Parents are always the last to know, Detective Wainwright thought to himself. "Good. We're going to send a car out to start the search. Maybe we can find some clues to where the boys are. I'll be coming over myself to investigate, and if you hear of anything, and I mean anything, please feel free to call me. Do you have the number?"

"Yes."

"Good. I'll be over in about an hour to inspect the scene."

"Is there anything I should do in the meantime?"

"Just sit tight. Maybe your son will call."

"Thank you, Detective."

"Keep me posted if you hear anything."

"I will."

As Peggy hung up the phone, she felt slightly better because she sensed that she was not alone in dealing with Chris's disappearance. At least now she had some help, even if it was the police.

What Detective Wainwright hadn't told Mrs. McKellar concerned a body that had been discovered. A surfcasting fisherman had spotted a body floating near Salt Meadow Beach, which was not too far from where the lost boys were reported to have been. Wainwright hoped that it wasn't one of the young men, but why make an already upset woman hysterical when he didn't have all the facts? First he would inspect the corpse and then head over to the Mc Kellers, Hookers, and Fairchilds. Hopefully he wouldn't have to ask them nasty questions concerning dental records or fingerprints. It was going to be a long day. Thank God, thought Wainwright, he had only three more years until retirement.

Peggy was about to light up another cigarette when she saw the lights from a vehicle pull into the driveway. It couldn't be the detective, she reflected, but perhaps there was some news. She heard the footsteps and headed toward the door. She prayed it wouldn't be bad news.

The door of the house opened, and it was her husband Tom. He had cut short his trip once he heard that Chris had not returned home. It had taken some deadheading on commercial flights, but when it came to traveling pilots have a way of getting around.

Peggy embraced Tom, and even in his exhausted state he looked so smart in his uniform. His thick hair slightly graying at the temples peeked from under his cap, and with a dark complexion and piercing brown eyes he brimmed with confidence. His appearance reminded Peggy of the days when they were first dating and when he had just returned stateside from the service. He had been a tail-hooker flying Hell Cat fighters off aircraft carriers in the South Pacific during World War II. He never spoke about his experiences over the Coral Sea. All that lingered from those days were some bad dreams.

"I'm so glad that you've come home," Peggy sighed as they embraced.

"Honey, I think ya needed a wingman on this one," Tom drawled. Somehow he never had managed to lose his South Carolina accent. "Any word on Christopher?"

"Nothing yet," she whispered.

"Don't worry. We'll find him."

Although he was putting on a front of brave assurance, Tom was just as scared as Peggy regarding his son's possible fate.

XIV

No matter how hard he tried, Teddy could not avoid the pain of the deaths for which he was responsible. The lifeless bodies on the beach would burn a place into the folds of his brain until the day he died. His beloved Mixer, the one unconditional friend he always had, was gone. Then there was the despised Lovejoy. He hated the man, but Teddy had done the unthinkable. He had killed a person, admittedly an evil man, but a person just the same, in self-defense but also in revenge. All he knew was that the act was wrong and that he needed time to think.

He reminisced about the times when Mixer was by his side watching Teddy put on his shoes and beginning the day with a game of catch. It was a silly ritual that had occurred for as long as Teddy could remember, a slobbery ball presented to him by an animal that moments before had been licking his genitals, but he missed that dog horribly.

Teddy tried to hide his tears. He had to be strong; he always had to be strong. He couldn't show Chris or Charlie that he was weak. He wasn't smart or likeable, but he was always tough, and his reputation depended upon that impression. He couldn't afford to be known as a crybaby, even by his best friends, because the perception of his imputed strength was all that Teddy had left.

Then there was Lovejoy. Teddy initially thought that he was done with him. The preacher no longer would be able to torment either his mother or him. His physical and emotional punishments were over once and for all, forever ended by the finality of death. Caleb Lovejoy, however, continued to haunt Teddy like an evil ghost that lurked in every corner of his mind.

In Teddy's dream that night the preacher's despicable guffaw of perverted pleasure as he wielded mastery over the powerless. As his dream lapsed into a nightmare, Teddy imagined that he saw a mud-covered Lovejoy standing before him. The only clean things on the preacher's body were the shining blade of the knife gripped in his fist and the Bible clasped in his other hand. The latter painfully reminded Teddy of the mortal sin he had committed. He thus was inwardly thankful that Chris had shaken him out of his slumber, thereby stopping the flash of Lovejoy's image and bringing him back to a place where he once again could think about spaceships that fly to the moon.

"You okay?" Chris asked.

"Of course I'm okay!" Teddy snapped.

"It seemed as if you were having some sort of nightmare," Charlie said.

"Fuck off, Charlie!"

Teddy rose from the makeshift shelter, revitalized by the cold of morning biting into his body. Turning his back to the clan, he unzipped his pants and began to urinate around the campsite.

"Wolves do this to mark their territory," he said. "That way they keep other packs away from them."

Teddy had to show his companions that he was not helpless. He was the top dog, and he was going to be the first to leave his mark. It didn't take long before Charlie and Chris followed his example. Then they all laughed at their spontaneous ritual in the chill of the morning.

Teddy looked around, trying to get his bearings on their exact location. To be honest, Teddy had never been much further than a few miles beyond Northern Shores. There was no way to get around the fact that the clan's leader was disoriented.

"I'm lost," He said. Teddy was surprised at how easily the phrase blurted from his lips, but it felt good to admit the truth. In any case, as his friends the clan would understand.

"I knew we were lost from the moment we set out on this half-assed trip," Chris joked.

"In reality," commented Charlie, "we aren't lost because, technically speaking, in order to be lost we would have no idea whatsoever of our location, and that is not the case. We know that we came from east of here. That fact is confirmed because the sun rises in the east and sets in the west. Therefore, we know that Long Island Sound lies to the north, and the direction in which we want to proceed is opposite to that of the Sound, and so we want to travel southward. That should bring us to our destination, generally speaking of course."

"Generally speaking? Are you sure that's the way we go?" Chris asked.

"Well, I'm not exactly sure where Grumman Aerospace is located, but I do know that it is south and perhaps slightly west of our present location."

A renewed confidence filled Teddy. He didn't feel lost anymore. Charlie had given him the bearings for his quest, and somehow he knew the way to go. In a few minutes the clan would be on its way to finding the spaceship that would land on the moon. First, however, one more thing had to be cleared up before they continued south.

"Guys, come over here," Teddy said, standing near the fire's dying embers. "We're all bound as brothers of the sea, right? I've always got your back, and you've got mine."

Teddy stared into the eyes of his friends, dirty faces with tangled hair. On the verge of adulthood, they all stank of wood smoke and unwashed bodies. Teddy knew that he shouldn't have to ask. Clan honor should never have to be explained, but he had to know for certain before they could proceed one more step on their expedition.

"Do you guys swear that you will never speak about what happened back at the hole?"

Chris stepped next to Teddy and put his hand out, just as he had done countless times when he swore to keep his silence. Chris had never broken the group's code of trust in and support of one another. The clan had its vow, and it was the glue of guardianship that held them together no matter what the circumstance. Confidential trust, a precious commodity of unyielding devotion, that every clan member held true.

"I don't remember a thing," declared Chris.

Charlie stepped into the circle. "We're all in this together."

Teddy completed the triad of stained hands and dirty fingernails. "We will never again speak of what happened back at the hole," he confirmed.

It was done. No matter what else might happen, Teddy had this pledge from his friends. He knew that he could count on the clan.

XV

Detective Wainwright had never been that thrilled with the beach. He was not inspired by sand or ocean water. Saltwater always made him feel unclean, and the particles of sand seemed to get into places where they didn't belong. As a child he was ambivalent about the shore, but after the Normandy invasion a beach brought back too many bad memories. He left his youthful innocence behind forever on Omaha Beach in France.

He refused to speak about the floating dead bodies to his wife or children. Those memories were left for the night sweats in the privacy of his bedroom. Red-stained seas, severed limbs, and the stink of death associated with saltwater soup were a heavy burden to bear for a boy of nineteen.

Private Wainwright lay on that beach pretending to be dead and watching as his squad, then wave after wave of others, get blown to bits as they leaped from their Higgins boats. He was always ashamed of his behavior. He had been sent to Europe to fight, but instead he had faked death, He had survived—that was all that mattered—but ever since Normandy he avoided beaches. His war was not an experience to be recounted at a VFW post or with family and friends. He lived with the shame of having been a coward. It was better that way, and it was better to stay away from the seashore altogether.

Detective Wainwright now had to walk at least two hundred yards of shoreline in the darkness before he saw a small crowd of people gathered around a Coleman lantern while a patrol officer kept guard over the scene. The rocks were slick with algae as Wainwright slipped and slid his way over to the corpse. It was low tide, and the foul smell of mud, seaweed, and dead crabs filled his nostrils. By the time he got to the location the detective was slightly out of breath, as he stared at the unavoidable presence of the corpse. The remains were obviously those of an older male, with his belly shot out by a close range shotgun blast. Wainwright was relieved that this was not the body of a boy.

Approaching the cop on duty, the detective pulled out his moleskin notebook and wrote down Officer Rhodes' name. He then showed his badge to the patrolman and was glad that the county had issued name tags to all of its personnel because he was so bad at remembering names. The patrolman was young, probably still in his twenties, and Wainwright could see that his uniform was pressed and clean.

"Who found the body?" he asked.

"The fisherman over here," replied Rhodes. "His name's Larson. He's a retired telephone repairman."

Larson had a ruddy and creased face from years of being outside. He was dressed in heavy green waders, and a ten-foot-long surfcasting rod leaned against the log on which he was sitting. Gazing out into the Sound, the fisherman had an almost tranquil expression on his face. A worn Dodgers baseball cap sat atop his head, and a pipe jutted from his mouth, as patient puffs of smoke instantaneously vanished into the breezes of sea air.

As Wainwright approached the angler, he saw a large freshly caught fish lying on the shore. "Nice fish," he said.

"The bass are running this time of year, but not like they used to."

"Mr. Albert Larson? My name is Detective Wainwright. It appears that you stumbled on this body while fishing, so what happened?"

"I'm afraid there's not really much to tell. I was out here fishing, just as I do every evening this time of year, and I saw this poor fellow here washed up on the beach. At first I thought it was just some washed-up garbage, but as soon as I walked over to investigate it became apparent that wasn't the case." Larson let out a puff of smoke before finishing his statement. "That's when I went down to the public beach and used the payphone to call the police. I then waited for them to arrive and showed them where the body was. That's pretty much all there is to tell."

"So, Mr. Larson, did you see anything unusual on the beach? Any hunters or other fishermen?"

"No, can't say that I did. At this time of year not too many people come down to the beach, and this isn't the place to hunt for ducks. They don't fly over this way very often. Of course, if it were goose season, you might hunt here, but you'd need a blind and a good dog."

"Okay, Mr. Larson. If you could stay a little bit longer, we need to get some preliminary information from you, so if you don't mind I need you to wait here."

Larson puffed on his pipe again. "Just how long do you think I'll have to wait here?" he asked.

"We need to gather as much information as we can while we're all at the scene, but it shouldn't take too much longer."

Most people would have been annoyed with Wainwright's vague response, but being retired Larson rather welcomed the excitement it brought to his day. At least he would have something new to talk about with his wife and the boys down at the barbershop, so he waited because he was curious about the deceased man's identity and because he could say he was first to find the body.

Wainwright then walked over to Officer Rhodes and said, "I need you to get all the preliminaries from Mr. Larson, like his full name, address, and phone number. Did you check the body for any form of identification?"

"No, sir. I was instructed to wait until a detective got here before I touched the body."

"Good job."

The words came easily to Wainwright, because the officer had followed instructions, but he dreaded going over to that body. The detective sighed and reluctantly walked toward the corpse. He prayed that he wouldn't have any flashbacks.

The victim was a bloated, pale, and balding man whose eyes and mouth had remained open with a vacant look stared into oblivion. In addition to a gash in his left temple, a shotgun blast had blown a six-inch hole through his belly. Otherwise the man was smartly dressed in fairly expensive clothes. It seemed to Wainwright that the man had been in the water for at least a day.

He momentarily looked up from the body and observed the flashlights of the homicide detectives coming down the beach. Wainwright could have stopped. He was just there to make sure that the casualty wasn't one of the missing boys, but his curiosity got the better of him.

Gently rolling the body onto its side, he could see a billfold bulge on the victim's right hip. Reluctantly, he unbuttoned the dead man's pocket and slipped the wallet from its location. He then made sure to return the body to its original position. Wainwright did this partly for forensics but mostly out of the respect for the dead.

"Rhodes," he said, "could you bring that light over here for a moment?"

The voices of the homicide detectives walking down the beach were getting louder. Wainwright briefly listened to determine whether he recognized any of the men behind the moving flashlights. He then opened the victim's wallet, where by a quick count he found at least five hundred dollars. Obviously robbery was not a motive in this death. The cash could be a tempting windfall that he could certainly use on his limited paycheck, but he wasn't that kind of cop. Digging deeper into the billfold, he found the little slip of paper for which he was searching—a New York State driver's license. Though smudged by immersion in saltwater, the name on the document was unmistakable: Caleb Lovejoy. As the morning sunrise rose from the east, Wainwright turned and waited for the homicide unit to arrive at the scene. He never liked loose ends, and this death seemed to have quite a few of them.

XVI

Teddy threw a log into the fire and watched it become slowly engulfed by the red glow from the flames. They had salvaged two cans of beans and some stale crackers from one of the boats in the yard. Steam rose from the partially opened tins as they were heated by the fire. The smell of cooking food, however meager the fare, was aromatic to the hungry boys. Chris could hardly control himself as he reached for one of the cans of sloppy sustenance. Lacking any utensils, he dipped one of the crackers into the can. When the food hit his taste buds, there was an explosion of culinary mastery unmatched by the most elite Parisian chef. Even though the beans and crackers did not satisfy the boys' hunger, they were enough to tide them over until the next day.

"How far do you think we've come?" asked Chris after the modest meal.

Teddy was stretched out on the tarp, his feet crossed and warmed by the dancing flames. Holding his head propped up against the wooden log, a blade of grass was gritted in his teeth.

"I don't know. Maybe ten or fifteen miles. Could be even twenty. We had a pretty good wind at our backs."

Chris began to poke at the fire with a stick. "Man, that boat sure can move. It's amazing how fast and far you can get in a boat."

Charlie remained silent during the conversation. His brain was calculating direction, wind speed, and landmarks such as lighthouses and LICO Power Authority smokestacks they had passed to come up with a more precise assessment of the clan's present location. With a stick he began to sketch in the sand a rough map of their progress so far. "Based upon my estimates," announced Charlie, "I'm fairly sure that we have made it to Cold Spring Harbor."

"Cold Spring Harbor? Wow, that's great! Where the hell is Cold Spring Harbor?" Chris asked.

"Does the phrase 'double helix' mean anything to you? DNA? Watson and Crick?"

Only blank stares appeared on Chris and Teddy's faces.

"Don't you understand?" said a frustrated Charlie. "Cold Spring Harbor Laboratory is where the biological key to genetic codes was first postulated. The three-dimensional structure of DNA was discovered not far from this very spot! Right across that body of water is where it all began."

"So what does that mean to us?" Teddy asked.

"It means that this is where we part. I'll go to the lab tomorrow, and you'll continue on with your quest."

Walking over to Charlie, Chris said, "You can't do that! You would be splitting up the clan. We all agreed that we were going to see a spaceship scheduled to land on the moon."

"Don't worry," answered Charlie. "I'll point you in the right direction, and Teddy knows the way to Grumman headquarters in Bethpage. All you have to do is to follow Oyster Bay Road to the south, and sooner or later you'll get there. Besides, I have to contact my parents so they don't worry too much about me."

"But you're the only one who knows the direction to get where we're going," Chris pleaded.

Teddy calmly walked over to Charlie. "Think of it this way," he said. "Wouldn't you have wanted to see the Mayflower before it set sail to the New World, or can you imagine if you were lucky enough to see Charles Lindbergh take off in the Spirit of Saint Louis before he became the first person to cross the Atlantic? Lindbergh started his quest right here on Long Island. We are so close to the history of navigation. It's something to tell your children and grandchildren about for the rest of your life. Imagine seeing the first spaceship from planet Earth to land on the moon. You can say that you saw it with your own eyes, a memory that will live with you till the day you die. Do you want to miss that? We have come this far together; we need our fire-starter to come along with us."

For once Charlie, the non-entity of knowledge, was at the forefront of the team. He became a key component to their location, a cornerstone of the clan's quest to see a piece of history in the making. A reflection of the fire's flames danced in his glasses as he thought about what Teddy had said. Suddenly, the clan's quest had meaning, as he pondered his next move.

"You know," replied Charlie, "it's highly unlikely that you will be able to get into the manufacturing plant at Grumman. They have armed guards, gates, fences, and dogs guarding the facility. You need some sort of identification to enter the plant, and even if you succeed Plant Five has a dimension of over 160,000 square feet. To give you an idea of the building's size, we could fit eighty houses into it and still have room to spare. We could wander around in that building for days before we even saw your spaceship. So realistically your ability to see the Lunar Excursion Module will be next to impossible. Besides, I've never been away from home this long before. Undoubtedly my parents are very worried by now. I'm sure that once I get to the Cold Spring Harbor Laboratory I will be able to find a phone and give them a call. That way they'll know I'm alright."

"Once you do that," said Chris, "our quest will be over. Everyone then will know where we are. The clan's quest will be over."

"Don't you care about what your parents think?" challenged Charlie. "Once this thing is over, I'm quite sure that my parents will never let me see either of you again. I mean, if we had told them before we left, maybe all this would have been okay, but not like this—not with what happened to Lovejoy. We should have stopped right there, got in touch with our parents, and told the police."

Teddy stood up and threw a rock into the fire, causing its hot embers to explode on the other side of the pit. "Shut up, Charlie," he said. "You didn't do anything, and you don't know anything. We all agreed not to speak about what happened in the hole ever again. It wasn't anyone's fault. I know how that bald bastard operated. He was going to kill us all, one by one, until he found where the money was. It was him or us, and that's all there is to it. If you don't want to come, you don't have to, but I know one thing: we won't have any chance of seeing a spaceship if we stop here."

"I think Teddy's right, Charlie. I mean," added Chris, "I think that Lovejoy was going to kill all of us, and, besides, you're the only one who knows the way. Without you Teddy and I wouldn't know where the hell we are. So you have to come with us."

Charlie took off his glasses and cleaned their lenses. Replacing his spectacles, he put his hand into his pocket and extracted a hidden article from his jeans. "You know," he confessed, "I cheated to get us this far. I've not been plotting our course simply by the position of the sun and stars."

Charlie slowly opened his fingers to reveal a round disk hidden in his palm. At first it appeared to be a watch, but the object had letters where numbers should have been and a lone arrow in the center. The red end of a needle wobbled back and forth until the instrument pointed to the letter N.

"You see," continued Charlie. "I had this all the time. That's how I knew where we were. If you know the general direction in which you want to travel and find a point of reference, you cannot get lost. It's that easy when one has a compass."

Chris and Teddy stared at the little compass, not truly believing in the power of a device that seemed so delicate.

"So how do we use it?" Teddy asked.

"Simple. We have a general idea of where we are right now. We know where magnetic north is because the arrow of the compass always points to the north. If we know where north is, then we know where south is. According to my best guess, this is Cold Spring Harbor, and we have landed on Cove Neck. All you have to do is to head south until you hit Bethpage."

"That still doesn't tell us how we get from where we are to Bethpage," Chris answered.

"Of course it would be better if you had a map of some sort, but you don't. Even so, as long as you can find a north-south road, you should be able to find the Grumman Corporation and, ultimately, your spaceship. You see, it's all very basic science. As for me, I believe my part of this quest should end here."

"What makes the needle point north?" Teddy asked.

"It's due to the spinning of Earth's molten core."

"What makes the core spin?"

"The geodynamics of the core."

"What are geodynamics?"

"I don't know, but I'll find out."

Charlie handed Teddy the compass, and Teddy studied the instrument. "Always a question within a question," he replied. "So all we have to do is to know where north is, and we should be able to get our bearings?"

"Yup."

One thing about Charlie, once he made up his mind. It would be almost impossible to change his opinion when it came to matters of parental influence. Besides, at this point they were all exhausted and desperately needed some rest.

"Why don't you think over your decision, Charlie, before we split up," Chris urged. "We've all come this far, and it's not that much farther to the spaceship. Isn't that right, Teddy . . . Teddy?"

Teddy was sound asleep under an appropriated Army surplus blanket that reeked of gasoline. Chris propped his head against a makeshift canvas pillow, his eyes heavy, and began to drift off to sleep near the dying campfire.

"You only have to go ten or twelve miles as the crow flies. The compass will show you the way," Charlie muttered as he rolled over onto his side and covered himself in a blanket.

To sleep under the stars when one is exhausted makes all problems vanish till the following morning. The things they had been deliberating would become issues again when the sun rose from the east. For now there was only the blissful amnesia of rest and sleep.

XVII

The morning was always the best time to get things done. Ever since Detective Wainwright could remember, he had been a morning person. The start of a new day was always fresh and clean, untouched by the turmoil inevitably boiling on a restless planet.

At least for now the morning was his, and he had had the night to think things over, to contemplate the clues and evidence. Of course, that was the problem: things just didn't seem to add up. Missing boys and a dead body—the circumstances could be coincidence, separate acts, but Wainwright had a gnawing feeling about it all. He had calculated the odds and probabilities over and over again, but two and two always added up to be five. So he realized that he wouldn't be able to concentrate on much else until the case added up to four and his world was back in order.

As he drove to the precinct past flat potato fields and the brown husks of cornstalks, the road was dark and devoid of life. However, that was the whole idea of his having moved out to Long Island from Brooklyn. It was to get away from the problems of the city and obtain the good life of the suburban dream, but it seemed that everyone from Brooklyn and Queens had the same idea. Wainwright could see the open space vanishing right before his eyes. Housing developments were starting to supplant the rows of plants, and farmland was being replaced by identical three-bedroom houses hundreds of times over.

Things were going to change around Suffolk County. He had seen it in Nassau County when Levittown was built—50,000 people crammed into a former potato field. Nassau was running out of space, and the city was starting to push eastward into Suffolk County. With more people there would be a need for more schools, more roads, more stores, more services, more crime, and of course more police. His job would be safe. As a matter of fact, he might even get a promotion by default. Yeah, growth was good.

The boys had been missing for more than twenty-four hours. After examining the body on the beach, Wainwright had gone to visit each of the families of the lost boys. The McKellar's and the Fairchilds seemed to have normal concerns and were ready to form search parties to find their children. Their worlds had stopped ever since the boys had disappeared, and he could feel their pain. He could see the worry in their eyes, but when he finally arrived at Mrs. Hooker's house . . . now that one didn't sit right with him at all.

By the time he got in contact with the woman, she had explained to him that Teddy was a child safe in the hands of God and that the Almighty would take care of her son no matter what "cauldron the devil concocted against her boy." Wainwright would leave such explanations to and priests and Popes. His job was to help God find the boy, no matter how safe his mother felt Teddy was in the Lord's hands.

There was no doubt that Mrs. Hooker was a stunningly attractive woman, though slightly disheveled, yet the more Wainwright talked to her, the more he realized that she was obsessed with

God. Every other word out of her mouth seemed to have some reference to the Bible, Jesus, or the Lord's blessings. Perhaps this obsession was understandable based upon recent events, but had this mania been focused on any other topic, Mrs. Hooker's sanity would certainly be in question.

The house was a mess with all those goddamn cats roaming around, climbing on furniture, and sprawling on the couches. No wonder, thought Detective Wainwright, the kid may have run away. Mrs. Hooker's POW husband is going to want to go back to the home-sweet-home of his tiger cage when he gets a whiff of this place. Even if the woman was a looker, Wainwright could hardly wait to get out of that dump.

For now, though, his number-one priority was to find those missing boys. When he asked Mrs. Hooker whether there might be any other place her son could have gone, she told him about her father's house. She explained that Teddy liked to visit his grandfather and that the detective might find the boy there, but she also warned him about Nathaniel's maverick ways. Wainwright then asked Mrs. Hooker whether she had visited her father to see if Teddy was at his house, and she had explained that with the finding of her husband she was busy getting ready for his homecoming and, besides, she couldn't go to her father's house because they were estranged. Evidently she hadn't talked to him in years, but she never stopped Teddy from seeing his grandpa because it would be unchristian to stop the boy from visiting him.

As he left the residence, Mrs. Hooker had advised him to make sure that his gun was loaded before he went over to Nathaniel's house, saying that her father had once shot at a census man. At first Wainwright thought she was kidding, but that was before he could see she wasn't joking at all. After checking in at the precinct, he was going to ride over to crazy Nat's. Of course, before visiting

Mr. Wells he decided it might not be a bad idea to visit the pistol range and brush up on his shooting skills. He hadn't used his gun since he had been on the force. Using a gun was like riding a bicycle—once you learn how to do it, you never forget—but it doesn't hurt to practice. Yep, when things ain't right, they just ain't right.

XVIII

C hris had lost all track of time when he awoke from a sound sleep. He could see Teddy curled into a ball by the fire, but there was no sign of Charlie. As he stood up to listen, he couldn't hear anything except the sound of the waves lapping the beach and the night's choir of chirping crickets. There were no footsteps or twigs snapping to indicate Charlie's presence in the area. Perhaps he had done what he said he was going to do and sailed away.

It didn't take Teddy long to get up once he heard Chris stirring around the campsite. He rose from his slumber looking almost like some sort of Plains Indian draped in a woven blanket. Hair askew and groggy, he meandered around the campsite aimlessly as consciousness slowly dawned.

"Where's Charlie?" Teddy asked.

"Don't know."

"Think he went back?"

"He said he wanted to go home, but I didn't think he would do it. I didn't think he would leave us," Chris replied.

Teddy shuffled over to the fire in stoic silence. Most people, he reflected, were a disappointment and didn't come through when he needed them. People just ended up in mental hospitals or were shot from the sky to disappear into endless jungles. Teachers were even worse. Exercising forty-three minutes of supervision five times a week, how were they supposed to care about him? And now Charlie was no different than the rest. It was painfully clear Teddy's dreams didn't matter to any living soul except himself.

Teddy did what he always did when things got bad: he said a silent prayer. He never told anyone about his prayers. Besides, Charlie didn't believe in God, and Chris . . . well, he just didn't know about Him. So Teddy slightly bowed his head and prayed silently to God to help him in his spaceship quest. Teddy would make one prayer at a time, one step in the right direction, so everything would work out for him, because God knew what the situation was in his measly little life, and the prayer, he knew, would give him strength to go on. He would forget what was behind him and strain toward what was ahead.

"Hey, Teddy," cried Chris. "Look what I found!"

His one-way conversation with God interrupted, Teddy raised his head and looked in Chris's direction. Poised at the top of the fallen tree was Charlie's compass, with its red arrow pointing to the north.

"I guess Charlie left it here. Is the boat still on the beach?" Chris asked.

Teddy looked toward the shore and could see the Intrepid tipped helplessly on its side. The craft was still in the same spot where they had beached it on the night of their landfall. Teddy stared at the boat for a moment and then turned his attention to the compass. He was not concerned with magnetic north, although that was the key to how the compass worked, but with the opposite direction. South was where they had to go, and he spied in the distance a large oak that served as a landmark for the direction.

"Where do you think Charlie is?" Chris asked.

"Don't know."

"Do you think we should wait for him?"

"Maybe for a little while."

"Do you think he went to Cold Spring Harbor Lab? He said that was where he was going. Man, oh man, are my parents going to be mad at me!"

Teddy kept staring at the oak. The reddish-brown leaves of the tree, affixed tenuously to the branches, falling randomly to the ground, floating aimlessly on puffs of cooling autumn air, with no with no place to fall, but down. He answered Chris in a flat monotone of disgust.

"So do you want to keep going or not?" he asked Chris, "because if you don't want to go on, it's okay, but I'm still going."

Teddy picked up the compass and carefully placed it in the top pocket of his shirt. He then grabbed some crackers, being careful to leave a few for Chris, and stuffed the rest into his jeans. After rolling up his blanket, tying it with some cord, and draping the bedroll over his shoulder, he resembled a war-weary Confederate soldier readying himself for a long day's march. He began to kick dirt over the dying embers of the fire, and grey smoke puffed into the chill of morning air of the extinguishing flame. "I'll give Charlie ten more minutes before I go," announced Teddy.

"Ten minutes? That's not enough time. What if he's out foraging for food or taking a piss or getting us a ride to Bethpage?"

"Ten minutes is ten minutes. If he's not back by then, I'm leaving."

The dilemma now for Chris was whether or not to follow Teddy. He was trying to stall for time, trying to make Teddy think about the foolishness of all this, trying to make him want to go back home before the whole situation would blow up into a thermonuclear disaster of woe for himself. If he went home now, maybe, just maybe, he would only be grounded until he was thirty years old.

"I'll bet Charlie is in the woods and found something to examine," said Chris. "You know how he always gets distracted with stuff. Probably something about the way plants photosynthesize sunlight or the way loamy soils percolate water through particulate matter or the fossilized leg bone of a Brontosaurus." Chris was amazed at what flowed from his lips, but hanging around with Charlie seemed to have some benefits for sounding intelligent. "Or maybe he's just taking a dump. I mean, that's got to take some time out here."

Teddy looked up into the heavens as he watched the sun's light of white and magenta pierce the eastern sky. "Well, if he is taking a crap, I hope he stays away from the poison ivy. I guess that I have about seven more minutes to go before pressing onward."

Chris began to look around the campsite to check on his belongings. "You know," he said, "that's your problem: you don't know how to compromise. Things don't always have to be your way. Maybe if you had taken a little more time to think things through, we wouldn't be in the fix we're in. Mixer wouldn't be dead; we wouldn't be lost; and you wouldn't be a murderer!" Chris hadn't meant to say it, but in his desperation the words slipped from his lips.

Teddy's demeanor changed in a millisecond as he turned his gaze from the sky to stare in the direction of his destination. A deep-seated anger flashed across his face when he realized that the act would always hang over him, no matter how righteous his justification of self-defense.

That was why he had to concentrate on the spaceship quest. The LEM was the only bright spot in everything that had happened of late. Quests are never easy. They are not supposed to be, but when the goal is finally obtained, to find something good in the depths of darkness, to see the chariot to the moon, then after that he could concentrate on what had recently occurred.

Teddy pulled the compass from his pocket and held it flat on the fallen tree. He would focus on the arrow pointing to the north rather than punch Chris in the nose. He watched the arrow wobble back and forth until it slowly fixed in one position. If Charlie and Chris didn't want to come along, so be it. He would proceed on his own to Grumman Aerospace, and somehow he would see his spaceship. Screw Charlie; screw Chris; screw Lovejoy. They could all rot in hell because his own mission was clear.

He looked again at the oak tree and lined up his destination. This time he found an object beyond the tree. It was a stand of cedar trees. The evergreens pointed tops piercing into the sky beckoned his arrival, and little forest was almost a quarter of a mile past his previous objective. He slipped the compass back into his pocket, sat on the fallen tree, and decided to wait three more minutes. That would be enough time for Charlie to return if he so desired, and after his last conversation with Chris Teddy almost wished that he wouldn't come on the quest either. Both of them were nothing more than a reminder of trouble. Let them fend for themselves.

"I'm sorry, man. I didn't mean to say it," apologized Chris. "I promise I'll never mention it again."

Teddy stole a casual glance at Chris but remained silent as he stared at the stand of cedars, his anger temporarily contained and buried deep. If he didn't acknowledge what had happened at the cove, could it be stored away forever? From this day onward he would always refer to the event as the "cove thing." There were many events Teddy treated this way, mistakes and mishaps that he stored in the secret passageways of his soul and hid from the rest of the world. So long as he could make others think that nothing mattered to him, the disguise of indifference would be complete.

As Teddy brushed himself off and prepared to leave, Chris pleaded, "Can't you wait just one more minute before you go?"

"I'll give Charlie one more minute," replied Teddy, "but that's all. When the rocket blasts off, there's no turning back. It just keeps going until the mission is completed. After the countdown begins, there's no turning back, all systems are go, and then you launch." He counted silently in his head, as the seconds until liftoff inevitably forced ignition, the final ten seconds ticked off without any sign of Charlie, he began to walk away.

"Come on, Teddy. Give him a chance. I'm sure he'll come." However, Teddy didn't even look back at Chris. "I'm sure he will be here any minute. He wouldn't leave us. He wouldn't leave the clan."

Chris began to gather his meager belongings and could feel the gravitational pull of Teddy dragging him along like aimless stardust as his friend marched off into the distance. Perhaps Teddy was right, he thought. Charlie was gone; his part of the journey was over. From now on Teddy and he would have to hold on to the dream quest as a pair instead of as a trio.

Chris decided that he would follow Teddy until he found a payphone at a deli or pizzeria, and then he would make a person-to-person collect call to his parents to make sure they knew he was okay. The tall brown grass of the meadow had punched down with each of Teddy's steps. It was an easy trail for Chris to follow.

XIX

Stopping his car by the dilapidated shack, Wainwright tapped the side of his jacket one last time to make sure that his pistol was slung snugly to his torso. As long as Nathaniel Wells didn't think he was a census man or from the IRS, a double-barrel shotgun probably wouldn't be pointed his way. Wainwright had learned that, when it came to fighting spouses or stepping onto a person's property, a law officer never knew what to expect.

Detective Wainwright had to watch his every step as he navigated the old discarded canoes, car engines and other junk strewn around Wells's acreage. The walk up to the door made him uncomfortable because there were too many hiding places behind nearby trees. If someone sprang out at him, he would have little reaction time to defend himself. These factors combined with the old man's reputation made him wary.

When Wainwright finally reached the dwelling's crumbling front stoop, he had to sidestep a decaying squirrel carcass compacted upon the walk. Knocking tentatively on the door, he scanned the house's corners before knocking again and shouting, "Anybody home? Suffolk County Police." He fumbled for his badge, making sure it was in his coat pocket, just in case he had to flash some identification. Then he tried the doorknob, which immediately opened the entry. How stupid was he, Wainwright thought, not to try the door in the first place? The slower pace of life on eastern Long Island was making him sloppy. Being from Brooklyn, he was always amazed at how many people never locked their doors around here.

Here, though, he was faced with a dilemma. Enter a person's home uninvited, and things could get ugly quickly. Did he want to have to deal with that alone, or should he call for backup? He made sure to leave the door propped open just in case a hasty retreat was necessary.

Wainwright could imagine the story on page two of the local paper: "Detective Ronald Wainwright, an respected member of the Suffolk County Police Department, was mistaken as a burglar and shot dead when he entered a Northern Shores domicile uninvited. The elderly owner, Mr. Nathaniel Wells, fearing for his life, killed the trespassing law officer. The home owner was found innocent of any wrongdoing based upon a home-invasion mistake.

"Detective Wainwright, the beloved father of two children, also leaves behind one very happily divorced spouse who will collect his full pension, even earlier, then either he or she planned. Services will be held at the End of the Line Funeral Home, whose motto is 'We bury them fast. We bury them deep. We bury them Cheap!' Don't forget to check out our cement statuary, and fine marble head stones, at Nudo Brothers Concrete across the street."

Wainwright could feel his heart beating rapidly as he again shouted into the apparently empty dwelling, "Hello. Anybody home?" There was still no reply as he entered into the claustrophobic breezeway into the small and extremely cluttered kitchen. Food was strewn everywhere, and he had to push his way through the space with a handkerchief over his nose to block the stench.

The abundance of disgusting flies in the room reminded him of the carnage at Normandy and the constant hum of insects hovering over body parts in the sand.

The detective stopped in his tracks as he turned a corner into the small living room and saw the unmistakable glint of a shotgun barrel. He knew immediately what he was looking at. The barrel sat motionless just a few inches above the floor. If Nat was at the trigger end of the gun, the old man knew exactly where he was. It was at times like this that Wainwright hated his job.

He immediately hit the floor, trying to make his profile as small as possible. Grabbing his sidearm, he realized the futility of his pistol against the firepower of the shotgun. At this range his gun was no match for old Nat's twelve-gauge. Given his position, he decided to take a conciliatory approach to this confrontation.

"Hello, Mr. Wells? My name is Detective Wainwright, and I'm here to ask you a few questions about your grandson. We were hoping that you could provide us with some clues to Theodore's present whereabouts. Any information would be of great help. Your daughter Muriel sent me over here." He said everything he could think of on the spur of the moment to make Mr. Wells sympathetic. However, there was still no movement of the ominous shotgun barrel.

Something was wrong. It was not humanly possible for a person to remain motionless for so long. Wainwright waited a bit longer before deducing that, if the person on the other end of that gun had wanted to shoot him, some lead and thunder would have commenced by now. "Mr. Wells," he said, "I'm only here to get some information about your grandson. The boy has been gone for almost two days now, and we want to make sure he's okay. Any information you might have about Teddy would be a huge help."

The detective peered around the bottom corner of the doorway to get a better look at his adversary. What he saw was at once reassuring and disturbing. Yes, Mr. Wells was sitting with a shotgun in his lap, and, yes, he was poised to blow the brains out of anyone who might enter that room, but it was clear from the old man's sunken look that he was stone dead.

Nat was sitting on the floor with his back against the wall and his shotgun gun dutifully draped across his lap. His face was ashen white, with every drop of blood drained from it. Rigor mortis had stiffened his fingers around his gun, as though attesting to his defiant nature. Wainwright could sense his resolve and determination, even though he had never met the man. It was clear that old Nat had died with his boots on.

Wainwright slumped into the dilapidated lime-green chair. Holstering his pistol, he fumbled for his pack of cigarettes. He could feel the tension slip from the room as his trembling hand struck a match. Wainwright tried to steady himself as the quivering flame found the tip of his smoke. Ever since the war his hands had never been the same, always shaking when he picked up his fork at dinner or signed his name on a document. He inhaled deeply and stared at Nat. Two bodies in two days. Maybe it was time to go back to Brooklyn. Things were getting a little too crazy for him around here.

As he glanced around the room for a phone, he noticed a note tucked under the old man's shotgun. Without a moment's hesitation he walked over to the body and retrieved it. He had been at many crime scenes, but rarely had there been a note waiting for him, unless of course it was a suicide note.

The cigarette dangling from his lips, Wainwright read the handwritten missive: "I killed that bastard Lovejoy. He was a no-good son of a bitch who hid behind the robes of the Lord with the title of a reverend to steal, rape, and murder his way through the world. He was poor excuse for a man. As far as I can tell, I done the world a favor. I ain't been the most friendly of folks to my fellow man, but I was always a straight shooter. And as I lie here dying, I just want to put the record straight that I done that no-good bastard in. If there is a God, I hope he has mercy on me.

Sincerely, Nathaniel Wells."

Wainwright walked into the kitchen again and found an old phone affixed to the wall. He didn't want to put the encrusted receiver next to his ear, and held it a few inches from his head. While dialing headquarters, he glanced down at the table and noticed numerous articles ripped from the newspaper concerning the lunar module that was being built at Grumman Aerospace. Normally he would have ignored them, but someone who had been at the ramshackle house was obviously interested in this particular topic. Why would so many editorials be ripped from the paper? Then he remembered that Muriel Hooker had told him about Ted's obsession with the space program and his wanting to be an astronaut. It was clear that the old man wasn't interested in such things. It was a hunch, but maybe Teddy was headed toward Grumman.

Now things were starting to come together. He had found a murdered man on the beach who was killed by an old man who just so happened to have a missing grandson. All the threads in this spider web of a case were forming a pattern. Wainwright knew more than ever that he had to find those boys to get some answers and to make sure they weren't hurt, or maybe worse.

XX

Teddy didn't look back as he traveled, continuing steadily on-ward. Chris, on the other hand, often glanced to his rear, in the slim hope that Charlie would somehow materialize from the brambles, and rejoin them on the quest. The three-foot-tall grass stems snapped with each step Chris took in a frost-covered mead-owas he headed to the wooded destination.

This was the perfect place for pheasants to hide in the early morning light. Chris was caught in the open between the place they had been, and moving on to the place they were going. He looked back one last time and whistled for Charlie in the hope that his friend had not returned home. However, there was no answer-ing signal, just the easy flush of warm air from the sea drawn upwards by the sun's rise.

Chris gradually caught up to Teddy by changing his pace from a walk to a jog. Teddy had stopped just short of the woods, removed the compass from his pocket, and was plotting his next line of site destination of due south. Chris was out of breath when he finally caught up to the instrument-focused Teddy.

"Just a few hundred yards away is an east-west road. If we head west on it, we'll come to a southerly road that will point us to Bethpage." Teddy put the compass back into his pocket.

"How long," asked Chris, "do you think it will take us to get to Grumman?"

"I don't know. It could be ten or twelve miles."

"Ten or twelve miles! That's going to take us all day."

Teddy walked over and leaned against a beech tree. "The way I figure it, if we walk two or three miles an hour, we should get there sometime before noon, as long as we don't get too lost."

"It seems such a long way."

"It's really not. I mean, we walk home from school, and that's got to be at least two miles, which takes us only about half an hour. Once we get to that road, we should make pretty good time. We might even be able to hitch a ride."

The one thing to which Chris's parents were adamantly opposed was hitchhiking. His mother had made him swear that he would never hitchhike, and most of the time Chris obeyed his mother's wishes. But this walk was so far that perhaps she would understand and make an exception to the rule. For now, though, they had to get from the woods to the road.

It was just a little stand of old-growth deciduous trees no wider than a hundred feet. It was a bit colder and damper in the island of trees, the moisture from the night, trapped from the suns evaporative rays, by the umbrella of branches of old-growth deciduous trees. Towering walnuts and oaks, their huge branches outstretched, were the last vestige of a once mighty forest. Teddy pushed his way to the other side of the trees as he stared at the needle on the compass, peering into the light on the other side of the woodland. From there he could see a road slicing through the meadows. It was only at this point that he felt they could reach their objective and complete the quest.

The road was no more than three hundred yards away, and Teddy knew that once they got to it progress would be much faster and less complicated. Oddly, a massive oak tree stood in the middle of the thoroughfare. The tree served as a beacon onto the next step, one of many small treks, that would comprise an entire journey, and with some luck and fortitude, would eventually sum into the quest.

It was colossal, an oak tree that was the king of the forest. Even from this distance the tree stood proudly, defiantly standing tall, to block the path of the twentieth-century traffic that passed beneath its branches. It was an Oak like no other, and the road's builders apparently had put their axes aside out of respect for a centuries-old tree.

"Chris," exclaimed Teddy, "look at that oak! I guess I just found my next reckoning point."

"Listen! Did you hear a whistle?"

The faint sound had emanated from a point behind them on the path they had just traversed. Teddy was inclined to ignore it as the wind trilling through branches, but Chris knew that it was a sound he had heard many times before. The whistle was unique to their clan: Charlie was signaling for them to stop.

"I knew it," said Chris excitedly. "I knew he wouldn't leave us!"

"Something must have happened to him to make him turn around," Teddy replied as he leaned against a tree.

"We have to wait for him. I wonder what happened to him."

"Don't know, but I wish he would hurry up." Teddy turned and gazed at the oak tree, choosing to ignore Charlie's pathetically slow trek toward them.

"Over here, Charlie!" shouted Chris. "We're over here!"

Charlie was loaded down with supplies. Blankets were slung over his shoulders and rope wrapped numerous times around his waist. He looked as if he were a hobo who had been out on the rails for months. Each of his steps resonated with the clanking of cans and containers swaying to the rhythm of his ungainly march. As he drew nearer to his friends, his disheveled appearance became more apparent. His glasses were smudged, his hair askew, and his normally pale face had darkened under layers of smoke and dirt.

"What the hell happened to you?" Chris asked.

"Well, it was quite simple. I knew provisions were in order if we were to continue with our journey. According to my best estimate, we have a ten- or twelve-mile hike ahead of us. If we expect to reach our destination, we will certainly need water to replace our bodily fluids. I managed to find a suitable container to accomplish this task." Pushing his hip outward, Charlie displayed a white plastic bleach bottle dangling awkwardly from his waist.

"You mean to tell me you've got water in that thing?" Teddy chided.

"Are you sure it's safe to drink?" Chris asked.

"That's the beauty of using a bleach container. Bleach contains chlorine which, as we all know, is an effective water purifier if used in the proper ratio."

"The Germans used chlorine gas in World War I to kill people," muttered Teddy. "If you don't know what you're doing you'll kill us all. It worked so well that they banned chlorine gas during World War II. Are you sure it's safe to drink out of your bottle?"

"If that were the case, everyone drinking city water would be dead. If my memory serves me correctly, the ratio is two drops of bleach per quart of water or eight drops per gallon. This is a gallon jug. By the way, the weight of a gallon of water is eight point three pounds, and it's extremely heavy."

"I'm sure I'll drink some of the water, so I'll help you carry it." Chris lifted the container and was surprised at its weight.

"Look!" shouted Teddy. "A truck! Maybe we can hitch a ride."

Teddy began to whistle and shout as he sprinted toward the red truck in hopes of getting a ride. The lone vehicle abruptly stopped just as it passed the oak tree, almost as though the driver had heard Teddy's shouts, but then it drove off, with little regard for Teddy's pleas.

Charlie and Chris clanked and sloshed after Teddy, momentarily forgetting about chlorine ratios. Meanwhile the unencumbered Teddy shot way ahead of his friends and was the first to arrive at the road. Teddy had visions of bumming a ride and speedily reaching their destination. It all could have been so effortless. Why would the driver stop only to move on? Was he another person trying to play some sort of cruel joke on Teddy?

That would have been no surprise to him. Teddy's whole life was filled with disappointments arising from the fact of just being who he was. This incident was no different than hundreds of other such mishaps in his short life. However, this time he snapped.

"You mother-fucker!" Teddy ranted. "You goddamn mother-fucker! Why would you stop just to drive off? What a goddamn asshole!" Teddy was angry at the guy in the truck, angry at his mother, angry for having to leave his grandpa, angry over Mixer's death, angry at the Vietnamese, angry at the world, but most of all he was stark-raving mad at Lovejoy for putting him in this predicament in the first place.

Running over to his friend, Chris said, "Try to relax, buddy. There will be other rides that come along, and if worse comes to worse we'll just walk."

Teddy would have none of this talk, however. He continued to shout, using every curse and filth ridden explicative he could summon. The venomous words spewed from his mouth, in a black fountain of hate, volcanically spitting splinters of wickedness in uncontrollable flows of linguistic magma. He then began to throw rocks and clumps of dirt in the direction of the truck, kicking at the ground in a manic dance of long-accumulated frustration.

Chris stood back, realizing that there was nothing he could do. He was powerless amid the storm and just had to let the emotional tempest run its course. To try to stop Teddy would only put his safety in jeopardy. It was much better to step back and look for cover, until the storm had blown out to sea.

Charlie, on the other hand, was mesmerized by the natural wonder that stood in front of him. It was an oak tree. By his best recollection a white oak tree, and was the largest, and oldest tree of that species he had ever seen. By his crude estimate the white oak had to be slightly over twenty feet in circumference, eighty feet high, and probably over three hundred years old. That meant the ancient tree had sprouted in the 1600s. It had been in existence one hundred years prior to the American Revolution and was a scientific gold mine.

He slowly walked around the massive trunk of the tree, observing the grayish-white bark flaking from its mammoth truck. The branches of the Oaks crown, some larger than trees themselves, arced over the road, with majestic arms of shade. However, the leaves of the tree were delicate in feature, not sharp and pointed, but rounded symmetrical foliage painted with red and golden hues of autumn, which pulsed through their integrate veins, ready to fall for the three-hundredth time in preparation for winter.

He walked over to the tree and reverently touched its craggy trunk. Upon closer inspection Charlie saw that the majestic oak had a hollowed-out center, and it looked to him as though a full-grown man could stand inside it. It took Charlie almost fifteen paces to walk entirely around the tree's base. There was no doubt that he had found one of the oldest oaks on Long Island. The hardwood was scientific discovery that was in plain sight, which the clan had miraculously stumbled upon. The quest suddenly took on new meaning for him as he realized that being tucked away in his basement reading books could not compare to the joy and excitement of actual discovery.

Teddy meanwhile continued his tantrum, and Chris gave him the opportunity to exorcise his demons. His mad dance was almost comical, though at his age this type of outburst would have been frightening to most other people. Chris and Charlie had grown up accustomed to this behavior on their friend's part, and they knew that with time his rage would abate.

Teddy took a few more steps and suddenly stood frozen, seemingly in a catatonic state, his head bowed toward the ground. Chris wondered whether he had had some sort of stroke or burst a blood vessel in his brain.

"Teddy, are you okay?" There was no response. "Teddy, come on now. Stop fooling around, okay?" There still was no response, only a blank and lifeless stare downward. Teddy's eyes were focused on something not more than six feet in front of his feet.

"It's dead. That's why the truck stopped. He had no intention of picking us up. He stopped because he killed a dog."

Chris ran over to the carcass. "The bastard didn't even get out of the truck. He hit the dog and just drove off."

The dog was a typically American mongrel with a tan coat, black back, and white feet. Its muzzle was long and pointed; small rounded ears drooped down the sides of its face.

"It's a female," Chris observed.

"The poor thing is all smashed up. One of its legs is busted, and there's blood coming from its mouth. At least it didn't suffer too long." Teddy wiped his nose with the back of his hand.

"So what should we do?" asked Chris. "Do you think we should bury it?"

Teddy bent down to examine the body more closely. "We can't bury it. What if its owner is looking for him? That bastard truck driver just rode off and left it here. Now I'm glad I didn't get a ride from that son of a bitch."

"Her tits are all swollen," Chris was about to proclaim when Charlie came up behind them and shouted, "Puppies!"

XXI

Wainwright made it to the Cove Neck Bathing Association based on a tip. The club wasn't comprised of very much and was quiet this time of the year, except for an occasional person walking a dog on the beach. There were two pavilions with a porch area situated between the barn-like structures. The white building was long and narrow, and it had a red shingled roof to add a splash of color.

The wooden building was boarded up for winter and empty of the small Sunfish and Sailfish boats used by the locals during the summer on Long Island Sound. The place had probably been bustling with people during June, July, and August when housewives circled their beach chairs to sunbathe. They then would gossip about children, spouses, and scandalous behavior as they sipped vodka-spiked lemonade, waiting until four o'clock when they would hurry off to prepare dinner for their commuter husbands returning from New York City. Meanwhile most of the bikini-clad girls and muscular high-school lacrosse players would be flirting on the beach. Wainwright had seen many clubs like this one along the shores of Long Island, but somehow he doubted that Charlie, Chris, and Teddy were involved with that crowd of kids.

The detective stared out into the harbor's expanse and groped for his nearly empty pack of cigarettes. This was the kind of place that his wife had been begging him to join ever since they had moved out. Wainwright had never seen the need to join a beach club. It seemed kind of snobby and stupid to him. There were plenty of fine public beaches that he, and his wife could visit free of charge. That was part of the tension in his marriage. His wife always wanted to join country clubs and beach associations so that she could mingle with the upper suburban strata, but he had been brought up in Bensonhurst. The problem was that somewhere between Brooklyn and Brookhaven his wife had forgotten where she had come from, and that was leading to troubles for a guy on a cop's salary.

Wainwright took a drag on his cigarette. These boys, he reflected, were too young to be involved in beach-blanket bingo activities just yet. They were still outsiders, limited by their inexperience and inability to compete with the older teenagers, but not children either. He deduced that these boys were in the awkward time of adolescence when dreams of grandeur had not yet given way to cynicism. The tip had come from a retired fireman who had watched the boys in their little boat to make sure that they made it to the safety of shore. However, he had chosen not to call the authorities right away because he didn't want to spoil the kids' adventure. After all, he had been young once too.

If only the tipster had known what those boys were mixed up in, Wainwright thought to himself. Their little adventure somehow involved a murder, and Wainwright knew the boys were an important link to a chain of events that had led to Reverend Caleb Lovejoy's demise, no matter what Nathaniel Wells's note said.

Wainwright walked from the pavilion area to the parking lot. A boat yard was on one side of the lot and an open stretch of beach on the opposite side of the pavilion. He was drawn to the cleared side of the lot. A large fallen tree marked the end of the car area as he walked up to the parking section's edge. There rust-colored grasses rustled and bent peacefully in the wind near the seashore. Then Wainwright happened to notice the charred remains of a campfire on the other side of the log.

He bent down and held his hand over the remnants of coals that had once been a fire. He was no Indian tracker, but the fire still retained residual warmth from the night's flames. If this is where the boys stopped during the night, they couldn't be too far ahead of him judging by the heat of the campfire site. The question was where those boys were headed.

When Wainwright put his hand into his pocket for another smoke, he pulled a newspaper clipping from his pocket. Teddy's mother had said that her son was obsessed with the space program. The clipping was one that Wainwright had found on the old man's kitchen table. The place it designated had to be where Teddy and the rest of the boys were headed. It was just a hunch, but the detective would bet a week's salary that's where the kids would somehow end up. The newspaper announcement read:

Grumman Aerospace Corporation
Family Day, 68
Sunday, October 5, from 9:00 AM to 3:00 PM
Rain or Shine!
For your safety and enjoyment please
heed the following directions.

1. Obey the plant security guards when parking.
2. Enter the plants in designated areas.

3. In factory areas, follow the marked aisles.
4. Keep children away from machinery.
5. Do not smoke in any of the plants.
6. Cameras are forbidden within the Grumman complex.
7. Do not carry packages or food.
8. Wear name tags and your Grumman badge.
9. IN AN EMERGENCY CONTACT THE NEAREST SECURITY GUARD FOR ASSISTANCE.

XXII

How can a boy resist a puppy? Charlie held two whimpering puppies in his arms. Their little bellies were swollen, and their markings were similar to the mother's coloration.

"How can we possibly take them with us?" Chris asked.

"We can't just leave them here," replied Charlie. "They'll die without their mother."

Teddy looked at the two helpless pups and realized that he had to help them while continuing on the mission of reaching Grumman. Somewhere in the back of his brain he entertained the possibility that these puppies might be a sign from God and intended as a replacement for Mixer, but he wasn't ready for that just yet. Not even Rin Tin Tin could replace Mixer.

"I guess we have to take them with us," Teddy reluctantly conceded. "Let me see one."

"Which one do you want? By the looks of the genitalia one appears to be a male, and the other is a female."

Charlie immediately handed over the larger of the two pups, which happened to be a male. Its fur was soft and dirty, indicating that these animals had been out in the elements for a while. Even the most hardened of souls could not resist the temptation to care for this little creature.

"How in the world are we going to take them with us?" Chris asked.

Teddy handed his dog over to Chris. "Somehow we'll manage," he answered.

"But how? They need their mother, and I don't know how to care for them," Chris said.

"I believe that mine has a bit of a flea infestation," Charlie observed.

"We've gotten this far. Two puppies aren't going to make much more difference," Teddy said as he pulled the compass from his pocket. Taking the male hound from Chris and shoving the mongrel in football fashion under his arm, Teddy proceeded in a southerly direction to the field-lined road. He knew that Family Days at Grumman ended by three o'clock and that if they were lucky they could make it around twelve noon, dogs or no dogs.

He began to walk, not knowing precisely where he was going but at least having a general idea of his direction. All he had to do was to keep heading south. Turning to Charlie, Teddy asked, "So if we keep going in this direction, what will be the first major road we hit?"

Charlie began to pet the head of the dog Chris was holding as he thought for a moment. "The next major artery should be Route 25A or, as it is commonly known, Northern Boulevard. Once we hit that road we should head west, and then at the next major junction head south once again."

"How do you know this?" Chris asked.

"History."

"History?" Chris echoed as he fumbled with his dog.

"I know it because of the American Revolution. During the war Long Island was occupied by British troops. As a result, a spy ring was formed on Long Island to report on British troop movements. After the war Washington used Route 25A to thank these patriots for their service. He went from Huntington to Setauket in a horse-drawn carriage to do so. Hence I know that 25A runs from west to east."

"Enough with the lesson," Teddy interjected. "We have got to get moving. Otherwise we will never make it on time."

"Wait," said Chris. "What about the mother dog's body? We can't just leave her on the side of the road."

Teddy heaved a huge sigh of frustration, put his puppy down, and pulled the mangled carcass off to the side of the road. Yanking the limp animal by its back legs, he immediately wished that he had some soap and water to wash his hands. An overwhelming sense of contamination engulfed Teddy, prompting him to recoil from the dog.

"Gimme some water," he shouted. "I need some water quick!"

"What's the matter?" Chris asked. "Are you thirsty or something?"

Unable to answer, a nauseous Teddy doubled over and vomited violently on the side of the road. He then crashed to his knees, totally incapacitated and helpless.

Chris knew that in normal circumstances they should immediately seek help at a nearby home, but there were none in the vicinity. If Teddy was really sick, how would they care for him? Suddenly his brain switched into a medical mode. In Boy Scouts he had been taught to stabilize, observe, and possibly provide some fluids before seeking further assistance. Lifting Teddy to his feet, he led him away from the side of the road and laid him down on a grassy knoll beneath the oak tree.

"Give me your blanket," Chris said to Charlie. "We need to keep him warm." Placing one blanket on the ground and another around the shivering Teddy, he contemplated his options. "Charlie, how safe is that water to drink?"

"Presumably, if my calculations are correct, it should be safe to drink. However, I'm not sure whether the water didn't cause Teddy's sickness, or perhaps it was something he ate."

"We all ate and drank pretty much the same thing. Do you feel sick at all?"

"No. I feel quite well aside from being a bit hungry."

"It will be alright then," concluded Chris. "I'm okay too. I've just got a slight stomach cramp."

Teddy, still a bit shaken, sat up of his own accord and put his head between his knees. The puppies were magnetically drawn to him, cavorting near his legs. Extending a trembling hand, Teddy was immediately distracted by the puppies as he began to pet them. An instantaneous bond had formed. He nevertheless was aware of the compass pressing in his pocket as he watched Chris and Charlie convene to determine the next step in their journey.

Already knowing that the sickness had vanished as quickly as it had appeared, Teddy was ready to continue with the mission. The prospect of seeing the lunar spaceship was enough to make him rise silently to his feet and pull the instrument of navigation from his pocket. Again he watched the needle of the compass wobble back and forth until it pointed to the letter N. As long as he knew the direction of magnetic north, he could go anywhere. This time it would be to see a spaceship, but in the future he could hike in the Rockies, go to California, or explore the Argentine Pampas as long as he had his compass.

While the rest of the clan deliberated, Teddy quietly resumed the trek south. Although they almost didn't see him leave, Charlie and Chris each grabbed a puppy and followed Teddy, not because they wanted to but because they had to see the craft that would land a man on the moon.

XXIII

The heavy reverberation of twin diesel horns drowned out all other sounds as a train pulled into the station. On Long Island, whether on the North Shore or South Shore, the drone of a commuter train is never far away, even on weekends.

Detective Wainwright's feet could feel the rumble as he sipped a cup of coffee in the deli across the street from the train station. He was hesitant to go to the pay phone to call Mrs. McKellar, he needed more information about the boys. Besides, he felt obligated to provide some hope to the parents, and if he had to choose which parent to contact, Mrs. McKellar would be the one.

The boys had made it past the rolling fields of parks and mansions, and finally encountered the unmistakable signs of suburbia—ranch, split-level, and colonial homes with two-car garages and quarter-acre lawns. Teddy had never liked these timid pioneers and their squares of neatly fenced yards claimed their modest piece of the dream. He therefore kept leading the clan relentlessly forward as he checked his compass, but he was at a point where he needed to get his bearings again. He wanted to find out just how far they had traveled and how far they yet had to go.

Teddy realized that all he had to do was to ask a local person about the remaining distance to Grumman Aerospace. With over thirty thousand employees at the largest company on Long Island, there was always someone in the area who either worked at Grumman or knew someone else who did.

"I think we might be lost again," Chris said.

"We're not lost," Teddy replied.

"Quite frankly," Charlie remarked, "my feet are beginning to hurt, and I would love to put Madame down. This puppy is getting quite heavy."

"Madame? What the hell kind of a name is that for a dog?" Teddy asked.

"It's a fine name for this animal," Charlie said defensively. "Having carried her most of the way, I feel that I should have the right to name this dog."

"Don't tell me you're naming the dog after Madame Curie?" Chris replied.

There was a momentary pause on Charlie's part for two reasons. First, he was shocked that Chris had deduced the true meaning of the name he had chosen for the dog. Second, he was dumbfounded that Chris even knew who Madame Curie was, and he concluded it was some sort of a wild guess by Chris.

"Well . . . I guess . . . yes, you are sort of correct."

"Sort of correct? I'm right on the money! Madame Curie was born in 1867 in what is now known as Poland. She was a winner of the Nobel Prize in both physics and chemistry. Ironically she died in 1921 from overexposure to the radium she studied during her life."

For once Charlie was silent, amazed as he was by Chris's unexpected intelligence.

"Wow, how did you know all that stuff about Madame Curie?" Teddy whispered to Chris.

"I have Miss Wilson's second-grade book report to thank for that information," Chris replied as he continued onward.

The puppies were starting to squirm and whimper from both hunger and the confinement of being carried. Likewise, both Charlie and Chris were getting tired, having hiked for almost two hours and at least seven miles. They had reached the town of Syosset, and though they were making progress, it was tedious and slow.

"How far do you think we've gone?" Chris asked.

"About five minutes farther than when you last asked that question," Teddy snidely responded.

"By my best estimate we have traveled close to eight miles based upon our current pace and time traveled," Charlie offered.

"So how much farther do you think we have to go?" Chris inquired.

Clearly frustrated by their slow progress and lack of precise knowledge about their location, Teddy responded flippantly, "I don't know. Maybe another five or ten miles."

"Well, which is it? Five or ten miles?" said Chris.

"Perhaps we should ask that gentleman in the phone booth about the Grumman facility's location," Charlie suggested.

"We don't need to do that," declared Teddy. "We're fine on our own, having come this far by ourselves."

"What name should we give the male dog?" Chris asked out of the blue.

"How about Leonardo?" replied Charlie. "I think that we should name him after one of the most brilliant minds in human history, Leonardo da Vinci, inventor of the tank, designer of a flying machine, and painter of the *Mona Lisa*."

"Why don't we just call him Dog?" Teddy muttered.

"Dog? Can't you think of a better name than that? I mean, there has to be a better name than just Dog. Hold on, wait a minute. I've got a stone stuck in my shoe. It's driving me crazy." Chris walked over to the side of the deli, away from traffic, so that he could remove the annoying pebble from his shoe, placing the as yet unnamed dog on the ground.

Wainwright was turned away from the road and the deli. Aside from calling Mrs. McKellar, he was contemplating telephoning his wife. His wife had never liked the fact that he sometimes worked on a weekend, and more than talking to her he just wanted to make sure she was at home. He would call to see how she was doing and ask whether she wanted to go out to dinner. That would be nice. It would be like old times with no distractions, just the two of them eating a candlelit dinner at the Italian place not too far from their home.

So he dialed his number and let the phone ring. The familiar staccato pulses of an unanswered phone buzzed on and then went silent. The first three rings he ignored because she was probably sleeping. During the second set of three rings, he surmised, she was in the bathroom or fixing her hair. However, by the twelfth ring he began to get annoyed, and a sudden anger flushed through his body.

He should have stopped there. He should have told himself she was taking a shower and hung up the phone, but he let it ring. After seventeen times and still no answer, he didn't know whether he should be angry or worried. Had something happened to his wife? Eighteen, nineteen, and twenty rings—had she gone out? She never went to church. Where would she be at this time of morning? After twenty-three times he slammed the receiver into its cradle and began to search for his pack of cigarettes to calm his nerves.

As the boys were leaning against the wall of the deli, Teddy pulled out the reliable compass out while Chris and Charlie watched the puppies play. Tired and hungry, Chris began to ransack his pockets for some change in the hope of scraping together enough money to purchase some candy and a soda, or if he was really lucky a roll with some butter.

"Do you think you have any spare change in your pocket?" he asked Charlie.

Charlie dug deeply into his pockets. Suddenly a grin appeared on his face as he fished out a gleaming John F. Kennedy half dollar. "I've been saving this fifty-cent piece for just such an occasion," he said.

"You've been holding out on us!" Teddy proclaimed as he snatched the coin from Charlie's hand.

"Hey, return that coin to me this instant. It's very special to me."

"It just became very special for us all," replied Chris.

"No, you don't understand. That coin is to be used to call home in emergencies. You see, I have epilepsy, and sometimes when I feel an attack coming on I can call home before it gets too bad. I already had one back at camp, and that was why I was missing for a while. It was a petit mal event. Nothing major, but enough to stop me in my tracks for a few minutes.

"The seizures come on more frequently during times of stress or lack of sleep. These conditions clearly exist for me at present, and normally I can feel them coming on before they happen. It's called an aura. I smell licorice and start to see flashing white lights. That's when I know the Evil Mr. Trips is coming for a visit. That's what my parents and I call an attack, the Evil Mr. Trips. We call a seizure that because whenever it comes on it's like someone sticking his leg out and tripping me. So you see, I use my emergency money to call home, and my mother will pick me up from school, or wherever I am, before I make a total ass out of myself. So now you know."

Charlie sat down on the curb and began to pet the puppies. He was exhausted but felt relieved. He had never told anyone about his condition before, but he sensed that Teddy and Chris could be trusted with his secret, and it felt great not to hide the truth.

"I have only one question," Teddy said.

"And what would that be?"

"Is your epilepsy contagious?"

"Of course not, you fool. And, by the way, I would appreciate it if you would keep my condition just between us."

Both Chris and Teddy nodded in agreement to Charlie's request. From then on nothing more was said about it. Their acceptance of Charlie was total and unconditional, and though they might joke between themselves concerning their friend's ailment, they would tell no one else about it. His secret was safe with them.

Peeking around the corner of the deli, Charlie turned back and said, "There's a guy in the phone booth right now, so if you want to call home you'll have to wait till he leaves. Hey, maybe he knows how we can get to Grumman!"

Wainwright lipped a cigarette and fumbled for his lighter. The doctor had told him to quit smoking because it was raising his blood pressure and might eventually cause a heart attack. Ever since the war, however, the addiction had helped him to calm his nerves. Cigarettes had gotten him through the ninety-five percent boredom and five percent inglorious panic that warfare involved.

He had known what it was to be cold, wet, tired, and frustrated. It was strange: he thought about the war just about every day of his life, but he never spoke to anyone about it except for occasional chit-chat with another veteran about the locations of towns and villages in Italy, France, Belgium, and Germany. Towns with names like Salerno, Normandy, Caen, Malmedy, and Essen. If there was one thing Wainwright had learned during the war, it was how to read maps. He had become educated about countries in Europe one town at a time.

Of course, the lessons were taught the hard way, marching on foot and hiding from incoming shells. As he learned the maps, he became intimately acquainted with the landscape—in trenches hastily dug into the ground, hoping to stay alive for one more minute, while advancing on Berlin to complete the job of winning the war so that he could return home. For Wainwright the war was about maps and holes.

Kids today, Wainwright thought to himself, didn't know what it was like. Protesting and burning draft cards—it was a disgrace. The whole country seemed to be going to hell in a hand basket. Finally finding his Zippo, he flipped it open and spun the wheel across the flint, but the sparks ignited no reassuring flame.

It was time for him to call some parents, but what could he report to them? He didn't want to tell them too much about was happening in the case. He knew that he was getting close to the boys, having followed them all the way to the beach where they had camped last night. How hard could it be to spot three boys wandering around a neighborhood? Looking out from the phone booth, Wainwright noticed all the children walking and playing outside. Then he realized how difficult his job was going to be, because it wasn't as if the boys were going to walk right up to him so that they could be found.

Chris was about to go over and talk to the man in the phone booth when an exquisite young woman parked her white Mustang convertible right in front of the clan. She was stopping to get a cup of coffee and was instantly drawn to the dogs. There is something about children and dogs that immediately appeals to the hearts of many young women, and this girl was no exception.

The boys watched in amazement as this beautiful blonde, her hair blowing in the breeze, with stylish sunglasses adorning her face, abruptly stopped her car in front of them. Without a moment's hesitation she bounced from her car and greeted them as if they were old friends whom she had known her entire life.

"Puppies!" she exclaimed. "Aren't they just the most adorable little things! I was out driving when on my way to get a cup of coffee, and I see these cute little things playing in the parking lot. What kind of dogs are they? Are they a toy breed? My Aunt May had a Shih Tzu once. These aren't Shih Tzus, are they? The Shih Tzu's name of my aunt's dog was Blondie because she had the most beautiful blonde hair we used to comb it and put it into little bows on her head. It was adorable.

That dog Blonde had a sixth sense about my Auntie May. That little dog knew whenever Auntie May was about to come home, and would run over to the door five minutes before my Auntie arrived home. Unfortunately, when it came to cars, Blonde didn't have the same ESP, that's extra sensory perception, and was run over by my Uncle when he was backing his car out of the driveway on his way to work. My Auntie, swore he did it on purpose, because my Uncle Jack never did like that dog, I can't understand why, it only bit him once or twice, in all the years they owned it. So where are you boys off to?"

"Well, Teddy managed to reply, "we were on our way to Family Day at Grumman."

"Oh, I love Family Day at Grumman. My Uncle Al used to work at Grumman, and we would go with him there. It was just so much fun. They had hot dogs and hamburgers, baseball games, and a adorable merry-go-round. My Uncle Al worked at Grumman for years and years. I think he was some sort of engineer. Of course, he wasn't like some sort of Choo Choo train engineer; he was the kind of engineer that use to design things, like air planes and such. He worked there until he had a massive heart attack about five years ago. He was watching a baseball game, or was it a basket-ball game? Well, that's neither here nor there. One minute he was cheering for his team, and the next minute he was slumped in his chair, dead as dead can be. It was a great shock to us all, most of all to my Aunt Vern, who was a sister to my mother and Aunt May."

Although he almost didn't want to find out, Chris asked, "Do you know how far away we are from Grumman?"

"How far? Well, you're not far at all from Bethpage. It's only about a about a ten- or ten or twenty-minute ride. I really don't know miles, only minutes by car. So from Syosset to Bethpage is about five or ten minutes. Of course, that depends on traffic. If you go during the morning hours when all those people are going to work, that ten minutes is going to turn into a forty-minute drive. It's shameful how long that ride can take. Traffic can be backed up for miles. Someone told me, I think it was my Uncle Larry, that over thirty thousand people work at Grumman. That's a lot of people, if you ask me. My Uncle Larry is retired now and lives over in Cutchogue. That's a funny name for a town, don't you think? I guess it's an old Indian name. We have so many towns with Indian names on Long Island. Patchogue, Ronkonkoma, Quogue, and even Syosset are Indian names. Nobody can even pronounce the names correctly. So do you boys need a ride to Bethpage? By the way, my name is Suzie."

The clan members looked at each other in amazement, hardly believing their stroke of good luck. True, they would have to endure the endless babble of Suzie for the next five miles, but they were willing to be a captive audience for an attractive girl in a Mustang convertible. They promptly piled into her car. Suzie turned up the radio, and they were off to Grumman.

It happened so fast that Wainwright caught only a fleeting glimpse of the car. The vehicle passed him quickly and without warning, but he studied the driver and passengers as they drove by him. He had seen pictures of the boys and could hardly believe his eyes as they slipped away, but he knew it was the lads for whom he had been searching. He now could call the parents and tell them that their sons were alright.

Hanging up the phone, the detective ran over to his parked car. He knew that a blonde female in her early twenties was driving the white 1966 Mustang convertible with New York license plate 7866-BN. He was missing the final letter but had enough information to find it easily. He only had to call a squad car, and the search finally would be over.

Wainwright couldn't believe his bad luck, however. Parked squarely behind his vehicle was a Little Lizzy Cupcake truck. Wainwright burst into the deli flashing his police badge and asking for the driver of the truck. An unshaven and balding man with a half-smoked cigar hanging precariously from his lips looked in the detective's direction from behind the counter. A stained and unkempt blue uniform clearly identified him as the delivery truck's driver.

"Are you the Little Lizzy guy?" asked Wainwright.

"Yeah, so what's it to you?"

"Your truck is blocking my car."

The man continued to toss his cupcake packages onto the shelves and deliberately ignored Wainwright because, although he hated his route, he had a job to complete and at least ten more stores to deliver his wares to before he could finally sit down and watch the ballgame.

"Listen, Mack. You'll have to wait a minute until I finish stacking my cupcakes."

"This is a police matter. Put the cupcakes down and move that truck!" Wainwright ordered as he flashed his badge in the man's face.

"I think you'd better do what he says," the proprietor advised.

The Little Lizzy vendor grunted an acknowledgement, knowing that an extra ten minutes had just been added to completion of his route, and slowly puffed his way out of the deli to move his truck.

"Do you have a private phone?" the detective asked the clerk.

"It's in the back."

Wainwright found the phone hidden under some papers strewn on a desk in the store's back office. He dialed the number to headquarters. He knew that he had spotted the boys, so his search was nearly over.

XXIV

It wasn't the first time that Suzie had been pulled over to the side of the road by a police officer, but it was the first time that she had been pulled over by such a handsome young officer. She had already found out that she was a sucker for a man in uniform, and she immediately began to flirt with the patrolman when she noticed that he wasn't wearing a wedding band. Thoughts of a church wedding with the patrolman in his dress blues flashed through her mind as she leaned enticingly toward him, trying to reveal as much of her cleavage as possible.

"Was I going over the speed limit," burbled Suzie, "or I did I go through some sort of stop sign? I swear I didn't even notice. I'm usually a very cautious driver. Most of the tickets I've received were for things not my fault. I mean, the time I got my speeding ticket was when a squirrel was about to cross the road, and it was either speed up or smoosh the poor thing. I never realized how fast a Mustang could speed up. Imagine, seventy miles per hour in a thirty-mile-per-hour zone." She fluttered her eyes slightly and flashed her seven years of braces-straightened teeth.

"May I see your license and registration, please?" asked the patrolman, ignoring Suzie's flirtation.

When she opened the glove compartment, a slew of papers cascaded to the car's floor. Suzie searched randomly through the jumble, thumbing through crumpled napkins, ketchup-stained menus, and scribbled notes while discreetly hiding her registration on the bottom of the pile. She was stalling for time in the hope that the attractive patrolman just might ask for her phone number.

Wainwright could see the flashing lights of the patrol car in the distance. The already congested road was almost at a complete standstill as Grumman Family Day attendees rubber-necked past a pretty young woman in a sleek car pulled to the side of the road near the facility's gates. He was glad that this whole chase would soon be over. Then the detective could get down to the business of discovering the connection between the juveniles and the murder, even if he was acting slightly out of his jurisdiction.

As Wainwright parked next to the Mustang convertible, he could not hide his disappointment. He had the car; he had the girl; but the boys were not in the vehicle. Flashing his badge, the detective walked over to the smitten Suzie.

"Did you give a ride to some boys?" he asked.

"They were the cutest group of boys I have ever seen! Did I tell you they had the most adorable little puppies with them and gave me one. Wasn't that the sweetest thing? They told me that the puppies' mother was killed by a truck and that the poor little creatures were left abandoned on the side of the road. They were walking to the Family Day event at Grumman, and I couldn't just let them hike all that way by themselves, so I offered to give them a ride. It was the least I could do because they said they wanted to see some sort of spaceship. My Uncle Vern told me that he saw a spaceship once, but we never believed him because he had a bit of a drinking problem."

"Shut up! Just tell me where the boys are now."

"Why, they're in there."

Suzie pointed toward the gates of the Grumman facility, but all that Wainwright could see was a mass of humanity, families with troops of children wandering around the grounds while eating hot dogs and having fun. At least he knew where the boys were, however. With a little more effort he should be able to find them.

As he reflected on how best to apprehend his quarry, Wainwright looked down into Suzie's car and noticed the puppy in the vehicle's back seat. Leaning over to her, he asked, "So did they tell you where they were going?"

"They said they were going to see a spaceship. There were three of them, all smiling and thanking me that I had brought them here. They were very sweet boys. They kind of reminded me of my Aunt Edie's boys. Did I tell you that she had six boys? That house was like a birthday party every day. You never saw a house in such disrepair, worn out by all those boys roughhousing in a little three-bedroom house. No wonder my aunt was subject to fainting spells. The thing that bothered me most about the house was the urine on the toilet seats."

Wainwright held out his hand, and this time Suzie immediately stopped babbling. "There's one more thing, that puppy you've got in the back seat of your car, he took a sweet duce on the back carpet of your car floor." As the detective began to walk toward the Grumman compound, he was stopped by the young patrol man.

"So what do you want me to do with her?" he asked.

"You married?" Wainwright responded.

"Why, uh, no."

"Get her phone number."

The Grumman facility was easy to spot. Large orange and white smokestacks thrust conspicuously upwards in the middle of the suburban landscape and looked out of place. Its power plant was needed to build fighter aircraft. Wildcat and Hellcat planes had been constructed there by the thousands during World War II. Grumman was widely known as the "Ironworks" for its production of aircraft that helped win the war in the Pacific. Later, during the Cold War, it had retooled for jet aviation, building fighters with such names as Cougar, Intruder, and Prowler that launched from the decks of carriers and extended the United States' military power to any point of perceived threat around the globe.

As the boys approached Grumman's gates, there was no mistaking that they were at the facility. A large blue sphere atop one of the taller buildings was emblazoned with the company's name next to its logo of a golden raptor winging its way into the heavens and a lone star.

The boys watched employees in cars packed with family members flash their ID as they were waved onto the property. The uniformed guards in their booths prevented all unauthorized entry. Clearly the clan lacked the credentials necessary to gain access to the plant. It wasn't as if Teddy had never infiltrated places where he didn't belong, but even he found Grumman's security perimeter a challenge.

"It looks like it's going to be pretty tough to get in there," said Chris. "I mean, besides not having badges, I doubt that they're going to let us in there with this puppy."

"It certainly seems to be a daunting task," Charlie agreed.

"Not if we use this." From his pocket Teddy produced a highly worn baseball, a relic of countless impromptu games. "Hide that puppy and follow me in. When we get to the guard station, just keep on walking like we own the place." Teddy nonchalantly then flipped the ball to Chris, and a small game of catch developed as they approached the gates. The moment they reached a guard, he held the ball and walked up to the booth just as a carload of unruly visitors was seeking to gain entry into the festivities. Charlie and Chris meanwhile ducked behind the car's other side.

"Hey, buddy. Where do you think you're going?" the slightly overwhelmed security officer asked Teddy.

A steamy station wagon, packed with excited children, impatient spouses, and incontinent grandparents, stopped by the entryway. The confused condition, added more convenient calamity to the situation, as the driver of the overloaded car and his spouse were in a sustained argument, and constantly turning around to calm a backseat of squirrely children, and overheated grandparents.

Teddy replied, "My baseball went through a hole under the fence." Distracted by the commotion of the children and parents screaming at each other in the station wagon, the guard waved Teddy onto the grounds. Charlie and Chris soon followed, shielded from view by the entering car. Through sleight of hand and deception, combined with a dash of assumption, Teddy easily entered the facility to follow his friends into Grumman.

The clan found themselves in an Oz-like land of festivity. Organ music from a merry-go-round blasted through the air as young and old alike went for rides on the spinning platform of outlandishly painted horses. The clank of cold steel resounded as men played horseshoes in pits of sand and wood. Games of baseball, kickball, and tag were going on everywhere as hardworking folks enjoyed a day outing at the facility where they were employed. To the three boys it was the culmination of an adventure well worth the hardships they had endured.

The first place they discovered was the food court. Sweating men in paper hats and dirty aprons freely dished out hot dogs, hamburgers, and potato salad. Charlie, Chris, and Teddy hungrily gorged on the fare. Simple food never tasted so good as they laughed at how they had inveigled their way onto the grounds.

Charlie attempted to hide his puppy and quickly moved it to some cover under the shade of an out-of-the-way tree. He shared his food with the dog he now called Zip, which seemed to fit its personality. Madame had become the property of Suzie as a token of the boys' gratitude for the ride she had provided. Teddy and Chris followed Charlie, holding overflowing paper plates of food.

A small boy approached Charlie and immediately noticed Zip. "They'll never let you on a tour with that dog," he remarked.

"What tour?" Teddy asked.

"Why, the tour of the aircraft factory. Everybody who wants to can see the planes in the process of being built."

Teddy immediately stopped eating. "Did you see the Lunar Excursion Module on the tour?" Teddy asked eagerly.

"Yes, we saw it."

"How do I get on that tour?" Teddy pursued.

"You just get in line over there," said the tow-headed boy, pointing to a sign block-lettered TOURS. "But, trust me, it's a lot more fun out here. And they will never let you into the building with that puppy."

Teddy stuffed some more food into his mouth, took a swig from his soda, and headed for the sign in a trance-like state. He was sure that the tour would allow him to see the spaceship. He turned and looked back at Charlie and Chris. "You coming?" he asked.

Charlie continued to feed Zip some hamburger meat. "Our little friend is right: we'll never get in with the dog. I'll stay here. You and Chris go ahead. I'll go on the tour when you get back."

That was good enough for Teddy, but sensing that something wasn't quite right with Charlie, Chris hesitated for a moment. "You coming or not, Chris?" inquired Teddy, and Chris, still eating, followed him toward the tour's start location.

Wainwright had gained entry into the plant and found himself in Grumman's security office. He was explaining about the missing boys to Lieutenant Kolchezch, a rather large and bald man who was wearing a highly starched blue uniform. Although cordial to Wainwright, he wasn't happy to see a detective on his turf. Once Kolchezch was outside Grumman's grounds, he was an ordinary Joe who had failed his county police exams. However, on this property he was in command, and he was going to make the detective realize that fact. Kolchezch was already in a foul mood because of Family Day. The visiting families were no fun to him at all, and he could do without all the commotion.

Wainwright placed pictures of the three boys on the lieutenant's desk. "These boys are on your grounds," he said, "and I need to find them."

Kolchezch glanced at the pictures, tilted back in his chair, and opened the Venetian blinds to his office. "I'll give you all the help I can, but it's not going to be easy. There are thousands of kids out there, and with all the festivities every man I've got is being used for crowd control. These Family Days are a security nightmare. I don't understand why they even have them. I mean, just about anybody can get onto the grounds. I'm sure there are some Commie spies infiltrating the place. How am I supposed to guard against that breech? The guys at the top must be out of their minds. And when they do find out that secrets have been stolen, whose ass is gonna be in the proverbial sling? So how long have these boys been missing?"

Wainwright wanted to roll his eyes in disgust, but he schmoozed Kolchezch because he needed his help. "I'm glad I'm not in your position," he said. "I can't understand why the higher-ups would do this to you. Mind if I smoke?"

Kolchezch pushed the lighter and ashtray on his tidy desk toward Wainwright. The detective pulled the pack from his pocket and offered a smoke to Kolchezch, but the lieutenant declined the cigarette he was dying to smoke.

"I haven't seen this many people having such a big party since the end of the war," Wainwright stated as he lit up.

"Yeah, I missed all that fun. I was on a destroyer in the South Pacific when the Nips finally called it quits. Man, was I glad when those bastards packed it in."

"I was in the Army in Europe," replied Wainwright. "I was never so happy as when V-J Day happened. There was talk that we were going to get shipped over to Japan for the invasion. I was damn glad when they dropped the bomb, damn glad."

Kolchezch opened the top drawer of his desk and pulled out a pack of cigarettes to join the detective in a smoke. Suddenly Wainwright didn't seem so crazy, and finding the boys didn't seem so nuts, because of what they had both been through during the war. He examined the boy's photos more closely. "I'll make copies and get them distributed to all the men on duty," he promised. "Don't worry. If they're in there, we'll find them."

The tour guide was a young engineer who had been persuaded into accepting such duty on Family Days. He wore a starched white shirt with a narrow black tie. In his top shirt pocket was a plastic protector crammed with the tools of his trade—a protractor, pens, pencils, and a small slide rule. His Grumman identification badge with an unflattering photograph dangled from his pocket.

The engineer's long black hair was combed neatly back against his head, and large horn-rimmed company issue glasses framed his pasty face. Had it not been for the owlish glasses, Albert Peats might have been considered a rather handsome fellow, but he was the sort who always had mechanical drawings of planes dancing in his head and could not be bothered with the distractions of outward appearance.

As Albert cleared his throat to speak to the crowd of folks readying themselves for the tour, he glanced down at his watch. It was the last excursion of the day, and he was performing this task primarily as a favor for a girl whom he secretly admired but who, without Albert's knowing it, had slunk off to be with her boyfriend.

Ever since the Vietnam conflict had been heating up, the Navy needed more planes, and so the plants had been working overtime to keep pace with demand. However, Albert was not involved with any of the plane-manufacturing endeavors; he had been assigned to the coveted and demanding LEM project.

His mind was challenged by problems unique to the vast and hostile reaches of space. Albert was constantly thinking about its airless vacuum, extreme temperatures, and rockets' navigational and propulsion systems. In the lunar module's construction pounds, ounces, and grams mattered so that the ship could escape Earth's gravitational pull. To deal with this problem, engineers made the walls of their LEM out of Mylar, nothing more than a fancy term for tinfoil. Truth be told, just a few layers of such flimsy foil were all that separated astronauts from the endless nothingness of space.

Peats had the distinction of being a Mylar specialist. He knew everything about its tensile strength, reflective properties, manufacture, and of course incredibly light weight. He had been working on the LEM for eighty hours per week for the past sixteen months, and a forty-five-minute tour was a welcome break from the demands of his beloved project.

Chris and Teddy waited in line as Albert stared at his watch to begin the 4:15 p.m. tour. He would wait no longer than the designated moment because being on time was extremely important. To be late for anything was a sign of either lack of interest or disrespect, so he would not wait one second longer to begin the tour, even if Leroy Grumman himself was coming to inspect the plant.

Staring at the second hand on his watch and counting down silently until it hit twelve, Albert Peats began his robotic introduction, even though only Chris and Teddy were waiting to take the tour. "I would like to thank and welcome you all for attending another great turnout for our Grumman Fun Day. You are about to embark on a very special tour of our impressive facility. Before we begin our visit, I have a few requirements that must be met in order to continue our outing."

Before the guide could continue, Teddy interrupted his speech. "Are we going to see the Lunar Excursion Module?" Albert glanced up and continued his litany.

"You will notice that to your right is a bin of safety glasses. For your own protection this eyewear must be worn at all times."

"Excuse me." Teddy raised his hand this time. "Are we going to get to see the LEM?"

Albert remained on script. "Please stay in the designated tour areas. Do not stray from the group."

Undaunted by Peats's adherence to protocol, Teddy walked directly in front of him and shouted, "Are we going to see the LEM?"

Albert briefly adapted his rote presentation. "Please, young man, let me complete my introduction. At no time are cameras permitted on Grumman grounds, and all camera equipment must be turned in to security immediately and picked up at the end of the day when you are leaving the facility. Any questions before we begin?"

"Are we going to see the Lunar Excursion Module?" Teddy asked.

"Hopefully, if there is time. Now, if there are no further questions, let us begin."

The threesome walked into the largest building that either Teddy or Chris had ever seen. The structure was cavernous and housed planes in all stages of production. Employees could be seen scurrying around the planes as if they were a hive of bees focused on their respective facet of the assembly process. Just then a man on a bicycle rode past the tour contingent.

"They ride bikes in here?" Chris asked.

"When working in a building the size of four football fields," responded Peats, "it's the easiest way to get around. Now I have to check in before we can resume our tour."

Albert knocked on the guard booth's door near the plant's entrance and mouthed to the guard inside that he and the boys were beginning their tour. The guard cursorily examine the youths. They had no interdicted cameras and were wearing the mandatory safety glasses. He counted all three of them and numbered the same in his log book to ensure that the same number of people checking into the plant would also check out as they exited the facility. Albert went through the formality of signing the record. "Last tour of the day," he said.

"Okay, see you again in a few" the guard responded as he glanced again at the boys and Peats. The guard was relieved that the tours were almost over and that come Monday morning life in the plant would be back to normal. As the small group trooped into the facility's interior, he cautioned, "Don't get lost in there."

Peats waved his hand as they disappeared among the fuselages, wings, Plexiglas, scaffolding, ladders, tools, and torches neatly aligned by each plane's assembly site. All around them men were engaged in building fighter planes.

An hour later another guard tapped on the booth's glass front. "It's time for me to relieve you," he announced. Placing some copies of the boys' photographs on his colleague's desk, he added, "If you see these kids, you've got to call headquarters ASAP."

The guard on duty examined the photographs and shot to attention. "They just went in. Call GHQ in case we need some help!" With that he stood up from his desk and ran into the plant to nab the wanted boys.

XXV

There was nothing worse than coming all this way only to get caught. It was a consequence that Charlie had chosen not to think about, and now he was being escorted like a common criminal to Grumman's security office. All he had wanted to do was to see a spaceship up close, and now the only thing he was going to see was the inside of his bedroom for the next six months.

The halls leading to the security office were barren and stark. He could hear his own breathing as the imbecile guard held him by the scruff of his neck. As long as they didn't think of him as some sort of juvenile Communist spy, a prison term would surely be out of the question. It was best not to say anything in such situations, he thought, but panic was beginning to build as he entered the security office. Charlie was seated in front of a stern-looking lieutenant.

"I was wondering where Zip is," said the boy.

"Who is Zip?" Kolchezch asked.

"He's my dog," Charlie responded.

Charlie, tried this tactic for two reasons. First, he was truly concerned where the dog was, and, second, it was a great ruse. If he could make them believe that he thought his apprehension was due to Zip, he would be in a better-off position than that of the suspicions concerning him. He also could divert attention away from Chris and Teddy so they could at least finish their tour.

"What's your name?" Kolchezch asked.

"Charles."

"Charles what?"

"Charles Fairchild."

"Where are you from, Charlie?"

"Northern Shores, and the name is Charles."

"I need your home address and telephone number."

As Charlie recited his address and phone number, Kolchezch wrote down the information. It was at this point that Charlie knew the jig was up. His infuriated parents would be there within thirty minutes, and so would Chris's and Teddy's.

"Where are your friends?" probed Kolchezch. "What are the names of the other boys with whom you came here?"

"Zip needs food and water, By the way, you haven't read me my rights. If I'm under arrest, what is the charge?"

"Son, you're fifteen years old. You don't have any rights yet."

Wainwright had heard enough. He stepped from the shadows at the room's corner and, hands in his pockets, leaned nonchalantly on Kolchezch's desk. He purposely said nothing and for a minute simply stared at Charlie in a parental fashion that made Charlie immediately uncomfortable. Wainwright put his hand in his coat, pulled a cigarette lighter from his pocket, and flipped his Zippo open and shut with an annoying click. Walking around Charlie, he once again disappeared from the teenager's point of view.

"Sonny, you boys are in a whole world of trouble, and I need some answers quickly, because if there is one thing I'm sure of it's that my time is valuable to me, and right now you are wasting my time." Wainwright popped from behind Charlie and leaned

directly into him, getting so close that the foul smell of stale cigarette smoke and body odor made Charlie sick to his stomach.

"I need some answers," the detective demanded.

"Answers to what? My friends and I walked here because we
wanted to get some free food and go on some rides. There's nothing more to it than that."

"Listen, sonny, cut the bullshit. I need answers to what happened to Reverend Caleb Lovejoy."

Panic shot through Charlie's body. The clan's secret was obviously not so secure. If this man was generally aware of what had
happened, who else knew about Lovejoy? His stomach began to
tighten, so much so that he felt as though he were going the throw
up at any moment. Questions began to flash in his head. Would he
be going to jail? How much did this stranger know? Why had he
embarked on this dumb trip? Would he ever see Zip or his parents
again?

"Charlie," pressed Wainwright, "I need some answers fast!
What do you know about Lovejoy?"

Charlie didn't want to cry. He didn't want to behave like a little
schoolboy, but he was losing control over his emotions, and if he
had no control over his whimpering, he would he would have to
tell because he wasn't a liar like Teddy. It was all an accident. They
had been fighting for their lives. He would have to talk to save
himself and the others. Wainwright would understand. Without
warning the strong smell of licorice filled his nostrils, and orbs of
white light began to flicker in the room.

XXVI

"This frame is the beginning of an A-6E Intruder," recited Peats. "It is a plane designed to perform close air support as well as deep strike missions. This plane can identify targets in all types of weather conditions at night or during the day."

As a visitor escort he had memorized the plane's specifications before conducting the tour. He knew the aircraft's wing span of fifty-three feet, overall length of fifty-four feet nine inches, and height of sixteen feet two inches. It was just enough information to sound like he knew what he was talking about, even though his current job had nothing to do with the plane.

"How fast does it fly?" Chris asked.

"It has a cruising speed of 414 knots, and a maximum speed of 563 knots."

Chris nodded his head as though he was impressed with the numbers. "How fast is a knot in miles per hour?" he asked.

Mr. Peats stared up at the ceiling as he began to calculate the numbers in his head. "The rough conversion is that one knot is equivalent to one point one five miles per hour."

"So how fast does it go in miles per hour?" Chris continued, being a little lazy about doing the decimal multiplication.

"About 647.45 miles per hour, or about 100 miles per hour less than the speed of sound," Peats confidently declared.

"Can we sit in the planes?" Teddy asked.

Peats was slightly unnerved by the boy's request. On all his other tours most folks were rather compliant with the tour schedule. "Well," he replied, "we're not allowed to sit in the planes, but we can look inside one as soon as we get to the finished product."

The end of the assembly line seemed to Teddy at least a half mile away from where they were standing. However, if he got through this portion of the tour, he surmised that eventually he would be able to sit in one of the planes and then see the spaceship. "Hey," he asked, "do they fly these planes in Vietnam?"

"Yes, they do."

"Do pilots in the Navy fly these planes?"

Peats again answered in the affirmative.

The aircraft now took on new meaning for Teddy. Perhaps, he thought, its type was what his dad had been flying when he went down in Vietnam. He stared at its bullet nose and the jet-engine intakes engineered precisely on both sides of the fuselage. He then examined the Plexiglas canopy that melded neatly into the aerodynamic flow of the A-6E. "Is the plane safe?" inquired Teddy. "If it crashes, will the pilots make it out alive?"

Peats looked proudly at the A-6E Intruder. "We take every precaution to ensure the safety of the pilot and crew. The Grumman Aircraft Company has always been known to take every precaution to ensure that pilots will survive almost all mishaps."

A lanky security guard approached them holding copies of the juveniles' photos as he inspected the images to verify that they matched the boys' faces. Confident that they did, he interrupted Peats's explanation of the plane's performance. "I'm sorry, but this tour has to stop."

"Why? We were just getting started," replied Peats.

"Don't ask me why. All I know is that these visitors are wanted back at GHQ. Now, boys, come with me." Speaking into his radio, he said, "Okay, I got em."

Chris could see the disappointment etched on Teddy's normally determined face. No verbal communication was necessary to convey the sense of defeat at almost obtaining their quest's goal. To be vanquished on the very brink of success was unacceptable to Chris.

When the security guard grabbed his shoulder, he snatched it away. "Take your hands off me!" Chris shouted. Not expecting such resistance from the adolescent, the guard temporarily loosened his grip around Chris's arm. While Teddy was pushed to the ground in the fray, Chris saw his chance and began to run away from the guard as Peats joined in the pursuit. Chris weaved around and ducked under the dismembered airplane parts, proving too elusive for the two men.

As he led this chase, Chris glanced back at Teddy in a fashion that told his friend everything he needed to know. It was a look that relayed the message, "Go find your spaceship. I will distract these infidels so that you can finish your quest." Teddy watched as Chris picked up a three-foot wrench and began waving it wildly at the men, holding back his adversaries with the courage of a warrior.

Further down the plant's aisle Teddy could see an army of guards running toward their position. As Chris continued to run, he ducked under the wing of a plane and watched as Peats slammed his head into it, temporarily taking him out of the hunt. Chris touched his fallen enemy counting coup, and held the wrench in his hand, stuck out his chest and bellowed a fearsome warrior yell, as he appeared to dance over his vanquished enemy. He beamed with pride, Turning toward Teddy, he then yelled, "Go find your spaceship!"

Teddy complied and began to run as fast as he could, looking back over his shoulder to watch as Chris created more diversionary mayhem, as additional guards showed up to the scene to focus on his friend's capture. He didn't know how long his fellow clansman could hold out, but his friend had given him a final chance to complete his quest, and so he ran. The last sight he observed was Chris's being overwhelmed, by the security personnel, with more coming in his own direction.

The fleeing boy had no reference point and was working without his compass. Seeing some large doors, he veered through them. The hallway was extensive and long. The noise of the manufacturing area from which Teddy had just escaped was now almost completely muffled as he entered into a never world of sterile dark silence.

Turning briefly to be sure that he wasn't being followed, as he entered another set of doors going deeper into the belly of the plant. He ran further down the hallway and through another set of doors. The corridor here glimmered on one side from the light of large observation windows. Teddy was joined by a man standing silently in the observation room, and as Teddy turned, he realized that the man was watching him intently.

The light on the other side of the glass imparted a mysterious glow to the man's profile as he stared at the winded and perspiring Teddy. "Trying to catch a train?" he chuckled.

Teddy was too out of breath to reply, but as he turned back he was immediately dumbstruck. What he saw in front of him was from another world. The room seemed to be more of an operating room, rather than a manufacturing plant. People dressed in sterile white medical gowns from head to toe were working diligently on an obviously special venture. There was an immediate sophistication to the project, that even Teddy's untrained eye observed.

Nothing less than the Apollo Lunar Module stood before his astonished gaze. The otherworldly craft was something out of science fiction. Four spider legs protruded from the bottom of the LEM, with large inverted saucers attached to the bottom of each appendage. What immediately caught Ted's eye was the gold foil wrapped around the lower half of the spacecraft, which reflected light from its crinkled surface. An American flag, its red, white, and blue colors, was prominently displayed on one side of the surface, and the words United States boldly written upon the other side of the craft, left no doubt to the Lunar Module's origin.

The top cylindrical stage of the craft, in contrast to the bottom half, was aluminized silver in color. Triangular windows stared blankly back at Ted like the large eyes of an extraterrestrial creature were observing into the souls of Ted and the man. Two prominent but small dish antennas sat on top of the structure, giving the LEM an additional foot to its overall height of twenty-two feet and a slightly lopsided appearance.

The man was calmly leaning against the rail in the observation booth and staring at the module with the same expression of awe as Teddy. "Hard to believe that thing is going to land on the moon," he said.

"It might not look like it, mister, but that spaceship is not only going to land the first men on the moon but also bring them home safely."

"Did you know that there are no seats in that bird. You have to stand to navigate her while looking out those little windows," the man added.

"It's all to save weight, sir. The Lunar Excursion Module has a launch weight of 36,244 pounds, and during liftoff every once counts, so the engineers at Grumman had to figure out unique ways to save weight."

Clearly impressed, the man walked over to Teddy and stuck out his hand. "Well, son, you sure know your stuff. I guess that if the engineers around here know as much as you do about going to the moon, we should be alright. My name is Charles, but most folks call me Pete—Pete Conrad."

Charles Conrad certainly did not look like the image of one of the chosen few to fly a spaceship to the moon. He was bald, short, and had a rather large gap between his front teeth. However, appearance didn't matter to Teddy. There was a charisma to the man that surpassed his physical features.

Teddy was mesmerized. Not only was he seeing his spacecraft, but he also was shaking the hand of one of the astronauts who was going to be flying into space and possibly to the moon. This man was a true explorer who was going to take on the challenge of man's greatest voyage. He was one of the chosen, and Teddy had just shaken his hand.

"My name is Ted," he stammered, "and it's an honor to meet you, Mr. Conrad."

"Say, how did you manage to get in here anyway? Shouldn't you be on some sort of tour? Are you lost or something?"

"I'm never lost so long as I have my compass," Teddy declared, pulling the small instrument from his pocket and displaying it to Mr. Conrad.

The explorer looked down and chuckled. "Well, you're not going to get too far with it in that condition."

Teddy looked down at his compass. The navigational tool was smashed and broken. During the scuffle in the warehouse the instrument had been shattered while in his pocket. Its face was obscured by splintered glass and its needle bent, rendering the device useless. Teddy's chagrin about his compass was hard to hide, but the objective of his quest had been amply fulfilled.

Pete Conrad looked at his watch. "Well, Teddy, it was an honest pleasure to meet you, and I would love to talk to you about this bird some more, but if I don't get going I'll be late for my meeting. Before I go I just wanted to give you something." The astronaut walked over to his briefcase, opened it, and pulled out a tiny green object. "Here, take this. It's a little better than the one you had anyway."

Teddy watched as Mr. Conrad started to leave the room, but before he did so he smiled impishly. "You know, a compass will work only when you're on Earth. It won't work in space, to navigate up there we use the stars."

"Gee, thanks."

In the palm of his hand Teddy held a D. W. Brunton Pocket Transit, manufactured by Wm. Ainsworth & Sons in Denver, Colorado. Upon opening the green case of the compass, he saw that the black face of the dial designated the four points of orientation with a bold white star indicating the direction for north. Small leveling gauges inside the compass ensured that it was level. As Teddy held the compass in his hands he realized that he would never get lost again.

XXVII

Soon after meeting the astronaut, Teddy was found by a posse of guards. He chose not to fight and went quietly, trying to keep the last glimpses of his beloved spaceship as peaceful as possible. The guard personnel promptly escorted him to the head of security.

Upon entering the office, he was met by a small crowd of people. Chris and Charlie were seated on benches. While the guards were providing details of the clan's capture, Mr. Peats was propped in a chair with an ice pack on his forehead to suppress the swelling of his head's encounter with an airplane wing. And, of course, there was Detective Wainwright standing in a corner and patiently awaiting his chance to interrogate the boys.

In all the commotion Teddy furtively flashed the compass to Chris and whispered that he had seen the LEM and met astronaut Pete Conrad, who had given him the compass. He then asked Chris to hide the instrument because he was afraid that he would be searched and the gift taken away. Chris quickly shoved the compass into a pocket of his jeans.

Lieutenant Kolchezch restored order in the chaotic room by ordering the guards back to their posts and sending the whimpering

Peats to the infirmary. There would time enough later to get these employees' accounts of the boys' capture. To Kolchezch the whole issue was that the boys seemed to be out on a romp and that, as long as no one had been hurt, disciplining the juveniles was a job for their parents. Of course, Wainwright would have none of that. He was going to discover what connection the group had with the Lovejoy homicide.

Wainwright had become extremely frustrated after his questioning of Charlie. He had tried every type of intimidation technique he could think of to make the boy crack, but Charlie was deceptively stronger than he appeared. The boy had recited the fourth and fifth amendments to the Constitution and used phrases such as "probable cause" and "being a witness against himself." The adolescent was better informed than most adults concerning his rights, and the detective had become somewhat apprehensive about his interrogation skills, especially when the boy demanded to see an attorney. Charlie had remained silent during the remainder of the detective's questioning. Seeing that his methods were resulting in littlie information concerning his hunch, Wainwright had chosen to return Charlie to the security office rather than risk a possible lawsuit.

The detective walked over to Chris and put his hand on his shoulder. "I need to speak with you for a moment, son," he said before escorting Chris into an adjacent cubicle.

Once seated in the small office, Chris immediately felt singled out and anxious. The artificial light in the office glowed with an unnatural shade of blue. Chris stared directly ahead at the blank walls as the detective slipped in and out of view. Wainwright circled his chair slowly and deliberately. Chris could hear his every footstep and breath. It was a very unfamiliar sensation for a boy who had never been in trouble with the law.

Finally the detective spoke. "You and your friends have come a long way. You know you have made your parents very worried about your safety."

Chris didn't know exactly what to say, so he decided to keep his responses short. "I didn't realize."

"You didn't realize? Oh, that's rich. You didn't realize that your parents didn't know where you were for the past three days? You didn't realize that you showed up some forty miles from home? You didn't realize that you gained illegal access to confidential government property? And most of all you didn't realize that you and your friends were involved in a homicide?"

Chris tried not to wince at Wainwright's damning barrage of sarcastic questions. Yes, the statements were all valid, but how was he going to respond to them? The particular problem was the last point about the homicide. How did the detective know about that? All the other questions were minor complications, but Lovejoy's demise was supposedly a secret known only to the clan.

Chris could feel a wave of nausea sweep over him. He wondered whether Charlie had divulged what happened back on that beach, had he broken the vow of the clan? The detective's inquiries left him off balance. There was only one recourse: he would have to play dumb and deny everything.

"So what happened with Lovejoy?" Wainwright asked.

"Who is that?"

Wainwright sighed deeply. "Let's skip the nonsense. I want to know who killed Lovejoy. I know that you know the full story of what happened to him, so give it to me straight. Your friend already spilled the beans." Wainwright pushed his face within inches of Chris. "Don't lie to me son. Tell me the truth about Lovejoy!"

Chris could feel beads of sweat forming on his temples. Had Charlie told Wainwright about what actually had happened or had he fabricated another story? The questions, began to swirl around in his brain. How had his day gone from euphoria to despair so quickly? What had happened to the warrior who had arisen within himself, and had now dissipated into a world of foolish dreams?

Chris's parents had always told him to tell the truth because lies led only to adverse consequences. Their adventure was getting so confusing and ending so poorly that perhaps it was better just to confess the truth, but then what about the clan's pact?

It hadn't taken Wainwright long to sense that he was breaking the boy. All he had to do was to press him a little more before Chris would tell him everything he needed to know. Once he solved the case, he would be heralded at headquarters, and, more importantly, his wife would finally respect him as being more than an ordinary flatfoot on the beat.

He could see the fear in Chris's eyes. After a few more questions, accusations, and lies about what he knew, the little twerp would be spilling his guts about the whole matter. When it came to things such as this, sympathy had to be abandoned, and the only solution was to subjugate the opponent.

Wainwright moved behind Chris, observing the boy without being seen. He remained silent and moved to the corner across the room. He watched the boy's shallow breathing, the tense posture of his body, and his straight-ahead stare, all signs of culpability. He could feel the boy's guilt. The confession was just moments away. Let him stew for a few more minutes, then go in for the kill.

XXVIII

All the parents showed up at Grumman's security office at the same time, and Charlie was never so happy to see his parents, even though he knew the deep trouble he would be in once they arrived home. Teddy's mother praised the Lord as she hugged her son and whispered what appeared to be prayers of gratitude into his ear.

"Where's Chris?" Peggy McKellar immediately asked Lieutenant Kolchezch when she and husband Tom entered the room.

"Oh, he's fine, ma'am. He's in an adjoining room with Detective Wainwright."

"Why isn't he with the other boys?" Tom asked. "And why would my son have to be alone while speaking to a detective?" Peggy challenged.

Just as Kolchezch was about to answer, Charlie collapsed in a convulsive seizure. The Fairchild's immediately rushed to his aid, familiar as they were with epileptic incidents. Kolchezch was instantly on the phone with the company doctor and after that called the local hospital for an ambulance. Muriel Hooker just screamed in horror. While Tom McKellar went to Charlie's aid, Peggy went across the hall.

When it comes to children and their mothers, instinct prevails. Peggy immediately sensed that her son was in trouble. She ran to his aid and surprised Wainwright with her forcefulness. "Why is Chris in here?" she demanded to know.

"Mom!" Chris shouted.

"He is here for questioning," replied the detective.

"Questioning for what?"

That was where everything got complicated for Wainwright. No formal charges had been filed against the boys; there was only an announcement that they were missing persons. The best charge the detective could come up with was that Chris had trespassed on government property if Grumman decided to prosecute the trio of juvenile offenders. As Wainwright glanced into the other room, he could see that one of the other boys was apparently having some sort of seizure. It was not his weekend. His wife was angry at him, as usual, because he wasn't home; the World Series was in process; and Peggy McKellar had the daunting glare of a protective sow bear in her eyes.

"I was trying to find out where he has been," replied Wainwright lamely.

"I don't care where he's been. I'm just glad that he's been found." With that pronouncement Peggy grabbed Chris's arm and marched him into the other room.

Once the boys had been found, Wainwright's case was lost. How could he prosecute a boy whose prisoner-of-war father had just escaped from Vietnam and another boy who was having an epileptic seizure? Maybe his gut was wrong, but it seemed better just to leave things alone, and so that is what he did, taking the easy way out in this investigation.

Wainwright watched the flurry of activity across the hall as a company doctor arrived and the convulsing boy slowly returned to reality. He observed simple joy in the lads face as the puppy was returned to his arms. The faces of parents relieved by their lost sons' recovery, so he decided to let this case go.

XXIX

Back on Planet Earth

Even after thirty years the compass held so many memories that I realized it couldn't be sold without Teddy's permission. For some odd reason Teddy gave Mr. Conrad's compass to me for safe keeping. After all these ensuing years I could claim it as mine, but I wouldn't do that. The right thing to do was to see whether Teddy wanted the compass back rather than my selling it to someone else.

It has been at least five years since I last saw Teddy, and even though we live just ten miles away from each other, we might as well be 10,000 miles apart. The last time I saw Teddy was when his mother passed away. It seems that she had succumbed to dementia, having spun off into a world of the Holy Ghost, and had often been found wandering lost in the present as she shouted praises to Jesus in psalms forever burned in a mind where all else was lost to the disease.

Soon after he arrived home, Teddy's hero father, was never quite the same after his prisoner-of-war experience in the sweltering jungles of America's lost war in Vietnam. Whether it was from buried post traumatic stress, or from the religious obsessions of his wife, he once again absconded to live somewhere in the deserts of Arizona.

Teddy never did become an astronaut. Instead he went on to study at Yale Divinity School and eventually became an Episcopalian minister. His specialty was youth groups. He is married to a lovely Scottish woman, and they have traveled the globe teaching the Gospel to children in some of the poorest parts of the world. I always knew that Teddy was the bravest of us all. In a sense he got to venture into space, just in a spiritual sort of way.

As I drove up to Teddy's little home next to a church, I saw him working in his garden, with his faithful dog panting by his side. He had lost most of his hair, but he still had an athletic physique. From the way he moved I could immediately tell that it was Ted. As my car stopped, he looked up from his vegetable garden, wiped the sweat from his forehead, and called my name just as a member of our clan should always do.

He embraced me, and it felt good to be home again, even though my mother and father had passed away many years ago. Ted led me over to a small trellised patio where a wrought-iron table sat under twisted vines of wild grapes and honeysuckle.

Ted's wife, Angela, then appeared from the house. She was a smart-looking woman with golden hair coiled in a bun and a lone curl along the side of her face. "So nice to see you again, Chris," she said. "Can I get you some iced tea or a lemonade?"

"Some lemonade would be nice."

She disappeared back into the house.

"Angela is a great gal," I commented.

"I know," replied Ted. "I'm so lucky to have her. I knew from the moment I met her on a mission in Kenya that we would be together forever. So, any news about Charlie?"

"Last I heard he was settled on a thousand-acre farm near Madison, Wisconsin, living off the revenues of a hedge fund he had created. Somehow he figured out, using computers and mathematical formulas, how to make money when markets are either up or down. The guy's a billionaire."

"Leave it to Charlie," replied Ted. "He's one of the smartest men I've ever known."

"So what are your children up to?" I inquired.

"William, a senior in high school and captain of his swim team, is getting ready to go away to college. It looks as though he will be going to the University of Iowa on an academic scholarship. Aidan is in the tenth grade and can be a bit fiery at times. I guess that she takes after her father. So how is your family?"

I didn't continue with the conversation, instead placing the compass on the table. It was still securely covered in the original leather case, with CONRAD written in faded marker across the top. Teddy gazed at the instrument as the breeze rustled through the trellised vines.

"Do you want it back?" I asked.

"No, you keep it."

"If you don't want it, I was wondering whether you want me to sell it. It's probably worth some money."

"Sell it? You can't sell it!"

"Teddy," I admitted, "I could use the money. I'm sort of down on my luck."

Ted put his hand near the compass, still unable to touch it. "I haven't seen this in years," he said. "I can't believe that you still have it. Could you take it out?"

I opened the case and pulled the rugged device from its leather pouch. The button holding the compass in place, snapped sharply as the compass was freed from the case. I slowly opened the metallic face covering, and the needle of the sextant danced wildly, until it slowly stopped, and aimed in one true direction. It still worked, the needle of the compass faithfully pointing north. Teddy picked it up as gently as if he were holding a newborn child. Staring at the astronaut's compass, he began to speak in very low tones that only he and I could hear.

"My mother shot him, you know. We didn't kill Lovejoy. Mother went to see Grandpa that day, and Grandpa told her that Lovejoy was after me and that it looked as though he was going to kill me. Mother came after me to save me. She watched me almost drown Lovejoy, but he didn't die in the water. When he woke up, Mother finished the job so that he could never come after me again. She shot him dead on that beach and left his body to drift in Long Island Sound. It eventually washed up on another beach. She let Grandpa take the blame because God was going to take him anyway. It was all part of their plan to save me."

Teddy almost went into a trance as he stared at the instrument in his hands while the memories rushed back into his head. Given all the changes in his life since those days, it was easy to forget what had happened so long ago. Ted had reconciled with himself with God and found forgiveness, but that didn't make the memories, whether good or bad, go away. He smiled and looked up at me.

"Remember when we snuck into Grumman? And when we camped on the beach? It was so fantastic to be young in those times."

"I got into so much trouble," I admitted, "that I couldn't leave the house for a month, and I think we didn't see Charlie for at least a year afterwards, but it was worth it. It was an adventure of a lifetime." We both began to laugh.

"You have to keep the compass for the clan's sake," Teddy whispered.

"I know I shouldn't sell it, Teddy, but I'm desperate. Ever since the recession I haven't been able to get a job. There's plenty of taxpayer money for wars and banks that are too big to fail, but none for me. At least if I sell the compass I'd bet that I can get about two grand."

Teddy was silent for a moment as he stared at the compass in his hands. It was worth more to him than the money that I was going to get for it. "How much did you say it was worth?" he asked.

"At least two thousand dollars. I saw some space artifacts on E-bay, and I think I could get at least that much for it. I mean, how many astronaut compasses do you think are out there?"

"Not too many." To Teddy the compass represented all that was good about his childhood—his mother, grandfather, our clan, and meeting Pete Conrad—and so he just couldn't let it go. "Wait here," he said. "I'll be right back."

I sat at the table and watched as Angela passed Teddy on her way out to the patio with glasses of lemonade. The ice cubes clinked as she placed the sweating glasses on the table.

"It is truly a glorious day," she remarked, taking in all the sunshine and blue sky. It immediately became apparent why Angela was so appealing to Teddy. "So where did Teddy scurry off to?"

"I don't know. He said he was off to do something in the house."

She sat down and began to talk to me about my hobbies, wife, and children. She had a great talent for turning the conversation around so that we were always speaking about me and never about her. So many people just talk about themselves and not about the people whom they are addressing.

As we waited for Teddy to return, Angela explained why she had to leave. "It was a pleasure seeing you again, Chris, but I'm off to the church to help with the secondhand shop. It's my turn to sell some of the treasures the congregation donates to the church. You would be surprised at what beautiful old things people give away. I've seen some lovely items come through the doors of that little store. I guess that certain things just don't retain their sentimental value for people." She stood and gave me a hug as Teddy returned.

"Where are you off to?" Teddy asked.

"I'm off to the secondhand shop. It's my turn there this month."

"Oh, yeah, that's right. I forgot."

She kissed him and walked briskly to her car. When she was out of sight, Teddy placed an envelope on the table and pushed it toward me before sipping his lemonade. When he leaned back in his chair and folded his arms behind his head, I could see the Teddy of our youth again.

"What's this?" I asked.

"Go ahead. Open it."

Inside the unsealed envelope were three five-dollar bills and one ten-dollar bill. The notes had a crisp look, but I noticed that there was something slightly different about them.

"Thanks, Teddy, but I think the compass is worth more than twenty-five dollars."

"Oh, I certainly agree with you. That's why I gave you three five-dollar certificates instead of two."

"I don't understand."

"Look more closely at them. Those aren't ordinary currency; those are silver certificates from the 1930s. Silver certificates were backed by the U.S. government in silver. If you turned one of those in to a bank, you could get its value back in silver. The country has been off the silver system since the 1950s. I collect silver certificates, and I figure that each of those five-dollar certificates is worth about $1,500 and the ten-dollar one about $700 in today's market. So, all told, I'll buy Mr. Conrad's compass off you for over $5,000. Does that sound like a plan?" Teddy reached out his hand to shake mine.

"I don't know how to thank you." I shook Teddy's hand and felt relieved that I could at least make that month's mortgage payment.

"If you would like, I know the president of Suffolk Bank. He told me that they are looking for honest people to work there. I can't guarantee you a job, but I'm sure that I can arrange a meeting between you two."

"Absolutely! I would love to meet him."

"Good. I'll arrange it."

As we clinked our glasses, Teddy smiled at knowing that a few of his grandpa's silver certificates were going to a good cause. Not only did Nathaniel Wells have a trunk full of money stored in the outhouse, but he also had some money lining the walls of his house, and hidden in the fireplace and, of course, stuffed in a mattress. Grandpa Wells may not have lived as if he were a very rich man, but he was, and he left it all to his grandson.

Teddy was glad that he could give something back to his fellow quest companion. Once in the clan, always in the clan, because there is always hope. That is a fact as sure as the tides that flow in and out from the sea. As sure as the way the waters rise and fall, as they flow around the sandbars in the middle of the creek, as they have done for ten-thousand years.